"Gre

"Our lives have [...] directions." Nikki sighed again, suddenly weary.

"Nikki, I never forgot you. I can still remember the taste of your skin, the texture of it. I still remember each and every time we made love, each and every time you moaned my name." He placed his hands on her shoulders. "Tell me you don't think about those nights under the boardwalk. Look at me and tell me you don't remember how right we felt together."

She drew upon the anger that was always just beneath the surface. She thought of her joyous letter to him, answered by an envelope of money.

She looked into his eyes and lied. "Never," she said firmly.

Dear Reader:

Welcome to Silhouette Desire — provocative, compelling, contemporary love stories written by and for today's woman. These are stories to treasure.

Each and every Silhouette Desire is a wonderful romance in which the emotional and the sensual go hand in hand. When you open a Desire, you enter a whole new world — a world that has, naturally, a perfect hero just waiting to whisk you away! A Silhouette Desire can be light-hearted or serious, but it will always be satisfying.

We hope you enjoy this Desire today — and will go on to enjoy many more.

Please write to us:

Jane Nicholls
Silhouette Books
PO Box 236
Thornton Road
Croydon
Surrey
CR9 3RU

Under the Boardwalk

CARLA CASSIDY

*First published in Great Britain in 1995
by Silhouette Books, Eton House, 18-24 Paradise Road,
Richmond, Surrey TW9 1SR*

© Carla Bracale 1994

*Silhouette, Silhouette Desire and Colophon are
Trade Marks of Harlequin Enterprises B.V.*

ISBN 0 373 59525 5

22-9502

Made and printed in Great Britain

CARLA CASSIDY

is the author of ten Young Adult novels, as well as many contemporary romances. She's been a cheerleader for the Kansas City Chiefs football team and travelled the East Coast as a singer and dancer in a band, but the greatest pleasure she's had is in creating romance and happiness for readers.

Another Silhouette Book by Carla Cassidy

Silhouette Desire

A Fleeting Moment

Prologue

She tossed restlessly on the narrow bed...waiting, anticipating...knowing he would come before the moon reached its zenith, before the sand lost the last of the heat of the day.

She sat up as she heard the familiar brush of fingers against her window screen. Heart thudding loudly, she left the bed, raised the screen and reached for his hand, knowing it would be there to help her over the sill.

Gazing at him, she swallowed a joyous burst of laughter, noting how the moonlight stroked his bold, handsome features. Without warning, she turned and ran across the sand dunes, toward the thundering waves of the ocean. She heard his laughter behind her and echoed it with her own.

Before she reached the tumbling waves, she paused only long enough to strip off the cotton nightgown. Then, naked and free, she dived into the waves. The cold water forced a gasp from her as it drove the air from her lungs. She surfaced, looking back to where he stood on the shore. He, too, had taken off his clothes, but she knew no matter how she coaxed he wouldn't venture into the icy waves.

As she swam, her gaze went often to him, the brilliant moonlight glistening on his darkly tanned, well-muscled build. He stood patiently, waiting for her to tire and seek the warmth of his embrace.

When she finally returned to the shore, he scooped her up in his arms and carried her to the darkened shadows beneath the boardwalk. Once there, he lay her gently on the sand, her body shifting to accommodate his as the sand beneath her displaced and molded to her form.

With the pounding rhythm of the waves ringing in her ears, he took her, his mouth tasting the saltiness of the ocean's tears, their bodies moving together as naturally as the waves meeting the shore.

Afterward, they remained in each other's arms. ''Forever,'' he whispered to her.

''Forever,'' she echoed, and with the passion and confidence of youth, there was no doubt in her mind that they would indeed be lovers forever.

One

——

Nicolette Young danced the three marionettes across the stage, smiling in satisfaction as she heard the laughter of the audience above the tape-recorded music. The giraffes always brought down the house, which was why Nikki always saved them for the finale. There was something so ridiculous about a trio of giraffes moving in sync to the latest popular rap song, that the audience couldn't help but laugh and clap their hands in appreciation.

Nikki looked over the top of the black curtain that hid her from the audience's view. Her gaze moved across the people sitting on the chairs, pleased to see new faces, testimony to the tourist season's having once again arrived.

She hoped the boardwalk had a good year. The past two seasons had not been so great. The country was in the middle of a recession and fewer people were taking vacations. Those who did, didn't choose to make Land's End, the boardwalk in Oceanview, New Jersey, one of their stops.

She continued to peruse the audience, her hands automatically performing marionette magic.

Then she saw him. A dull roaring resounded in her ears. She faltered, the three giraffes on stage doing impromptu nosedives. The audience laughed, assuming it was all part of the act.

Nikki immediately recovered, her hands continuing the crazy dance through sheer habit, while her mind went momentarily blank as she stared at the man who was a specter from her past.

Why hasn't he aged? she wondered wildly as she gazed at his handsome, sharply defined features. Like the picture of Dorian Gray, Greyson Blakemore looked exactly as he had the last time she'd seen him almost seven years ago.

His hair was the same midnight black, although shorter than she remembered. She knew his eyes would be smoldering chunks of charcoal, eyes that had always managed to heat her from within by a single glance.

What's he doing here? What could he possibly want? All kinds of questions popped into her mind, whirling around with dizzying speed.

So much time had passed, so many memories burned in her brain . . . good memories, bittersweet ones . . . and ones that tormented her. She shook herself, surprised to realize that unconsciously she'd managed to end the show by rote. She punched the button that drew the curtain across the front of the stage, vaguely aware of her tape-recorded voice announcing the time of the next performance.

She carefully pulled the giraffe marionettes over the top of the backdrop and hung them on the holders where they would be ready for the following show. She was vaguely conscious of the sounds of shuffling feet, youthful chattering as the audience exited the theater.

Her mind was curiously numb, her thoughts confused as she straightened each thin wire on each puppet with meticulous care. Had she remembered to lock her front door when she'd left that morning? Maybe it hadn't been him at all, only somebody who resembled Grey. Had she shut off the coffeemaker before leaving the house earlier? Perhaps he had only been a figment of her imagination.

"Nikki?"

The low deep voice came from the audience side of the stage. Nikki closed her eyes, a shiver dancing up her spine. Was it possible that a figment of her imagination had vocal chords?

"Nicolette Richards?"

Ah yes, it was Greyson, all right. Nobody else had ever been able to say her name in quite the way he did, a way which always stirred something deep within her.

Taking a deep breath, she stepped out from behind the stage and faced the man she'd once loved, the man who had betrayed her in the worst possible way.

"Hello, Grey." She was pleased to hear that her voice sounded cool, well modulated, not reflecting the tumultuous emotions that pressed thickly in her chest at the sight of him.

"I enjoyed the show. You've always been so wonderfully talented." His voice was equally controlled, no sign that there was any emotional tug at all in seeing her again. She hated him for that.

How civil we are, she thought, staring at him wordlessly. How polite and kind, like two people meeting for the very first time.

She had been mistaken in that brief moment she'd seen him over the top of the background curtain. He had aged. The lines of the last seven years radiated from the corners of his dark eyes and deepened the creases on either side of his sensuous mouth. A few premature silver hairs glistened at his temples. The last time she'd seen him, he'd been only eighteen, and now, at twenty-five, the promising attractiveness had matured into full-blown handsome. Somehow, this provoked irritation in Nikki.

"What are you doing here, Grey?" she asked, aggravated that after all that had happened between them, despite the bitterness she felt toward him, she could still remember the taste of his kisses, the feel of his hands against her heated naked flesh. She was suddenly aware of a crackling electricity in the air surrounding them.

"I need to talk to you." His voice was flat, his face expressionless.

Nikki stared at him curiously. What could he possibly want to talk to her about? And where the hell had he been when she had needed him seven years ago?

Suddenly, she wanted to be outside, out of the confines of the theater, someplace where Grey's presence wasn't so overwhelming. "We can talk outside," she said, moving past him and out into the sultry night air.

She was conscious of him following close behind, and when she turned to face him, she realized what it was that seemed so different about him. It wasn't the passage of time that was evident on his face, no, it was the way he was dressed. The Grey of her past had been a sun-bronzed young man who went shirtless, wearing only a pair of faded cutoff jean shorts and a carefree smile.

The man before her wore a well-tailored suit and expensive leather shoes. More than that, he wore the Blakemore air of arrogance and confidence.

"What do you need to talk to me about?" she asked, wishing that he'd never come back, that they hadn't shared a past so intense it remained in her soul in vivid detail.

"You probably heard that my father passed away," he began.

Nikki nodded. "I was sorry to hear about it," she said, but they were just empty words without the warmth of any real emotion behind them. Grey's father had been a harsh, sanctimonious man who'd made it clear from the beginning that he didn't like her. A "boardwalk brat" wasn't a fit companion for a Blakemore.

She looked at Grey, waiting for him to continue, noting how the colorful lights strung along the boardwalk reflected in the darkness of his hair. She had once loved to stroke the silken strands, feel the richness between her fingers. She now clenched her hands tightly shut, feeling her nails dig into her palms.

He moved over to the edge of the wooden walk-way and leaned against the railing. Beyond him the ocean pounded the shore, the waves silver-tipped with the light spilling from the full moon. "I've moved back here to take over the family business. Since most of that business interest lies on the boardwalk, I decided it was important I talk to you. You've always seemed to have a finger on the pulse of the area.''

"What do you want to know?" she asked stiffly.

"From all indications, Land's End is slowly dying.''

"We've had a couple of rough years," she agreed reluctantly. "But we're anticipating this season will be much better.''

"We've received an offer on the place.''

Nikki narrowed her eyes. Yes, she'd heard the rumors that a large developer was interested in buying the area and putting up a luxury hotel. "Are you going to accept it?'' Her heart seemed to pause in its beating as she waited for his answer.

He looked out somewhere in the distance, his eyes as dark and impenetrable as the ocean's depths. "I haven't made up my mind yet.''

Nikki took a deep breath, trying to swallow the anger that welled up inside her, an anger she knew was not only generated from this moment, but from the past, insidious in its strength. "If you sell Land's End, you'll be making a lot of people homeless.''

His nostrils thinned and his jaw knotted visibly. "I'm here to assess the situation and make a decision that will be the best for everyone concerned.''

Nikki snorted a bitter burst of disbelief. "I'm sure whatever you decide, it will definitely serve the Blakemore interests."

He turned his gaze back at her, his eyes those of a stranger. "Had that been the case, I would have already signed the papers for the sale to go through. I wouldn't be standing here with you."

"So why *are* you here?" Nikki asked impatiently. She found it difficult to breathe, difficult to think with him standing so close. She could smell his after-shave, a pleasant scent of cool spice, a spice that evoked distant memories she now found abhorrent.

"I'd like you to set up a meeting with the others to discuss the future of Land's End."

"When?"

He shrugged his broad shoulders. "Whenever it's convenient for all of you. You can give me a call at the house when you've arranged it."

Nikki merely nodded, unable to speak for a moment as once again memories swept over her, bringing with them bitterness, anger and the aching memory of what they'd once been to each other.

"I'll expect to hear from you soon." Again she nodded her reply, and Grey turned and walked away.

Nikki watched him until he disappeared from sight, then she slumped against the wooden railing, her hands covering her face.

She shivered, allowing her mind to propel her backward in time, unable to prevent the memories that spilled through her head.

"You and me against the world, kid." How many times had she heard that from Grey when she was young? Greyson Blakemore, alienated from the other kids because of his family wealth. And Nikki, child of the boardwalk. The two of them had first met on the boardwalk's carousel. Nikki had been eight, and Grey nine. Immediately, they had confronted each other warily, both wanting to ride the silver steed with the bright blue ribbons.

"You're a boardwalk brat," Grey had said, obviously mouthing a term he'd heard but didn't quite understand.

Nikki had faced him squarely, unafraid of his bigger size. "And your mother is a girdle-squeezed, money-grabbing bitch," she'd countered.

For a long moment, the two had stared at each other, neither denying the other's words, but unsure what to do next. Finally, it was Grey who had broken the impasse. "We could take turns," he suggested, eyeing the silver horse longingly.

It had been the beginning of a relationship that had lasted from the end of May to the beginning of September every year. Nikki had lived for the summers when she and Grey were free to wander the boardwalk, playing hide-and-seek beneath the wooden piers, and later learning other, more exciting games to play when the darkness of the evening descended and the heat of those summer nights surrounded them.

When Nikki was ten, Grey was her best friend. At thirteen, he'd been her hero, and at sixteen he became her lover, and they talked of a future together forever.

"Nikki? Nikki, are you all right?"

The feminine voice pulled Nikki from the warmth of yesterday and back to the stark reality of the present. She withdrew her hands from her face and turned to see Bridget, her petite face creased with worry. "I'm fine." Nikki forced a smile.

"I saw him, Nikki. I saw him talking to you. Are you sure you're all right?"

Nikki nodded, releasing a shuddery sigh. She walked over to a nearby bench and sat down, afraid her legs wouldn't hold her any longer. Bridget joined her on the bench, her feet dangling in the air like those of a small child.

Bridget had been born a little person at a time when people had no real understanding of dwarfism. She had come to the boardwalk twenty years ago and opened a pizza place. Here, in the surreal atmosphere and carnival gaiety, like so many of life's outcasts, Bridget had found acceptance. She had also become a very special person in Nikki's life.

"Did he say anything...about the baby?" she said, taking Nikki's hand in hers.

Nikki shook her head and closed her eyes against the stab of pain that pierced through her...a pain of emptiness and loss. "I can't tell you how many times I've imagined seeing him," Nikki said softly, looking at Bridget once again. "So many nights I fantasized about his return, rehearsed all the things I wanted to say—" She stopped in frustration, unable to explain how when actually facing him, she couldn't think of anything except the reality of his presence. "He called me Nicolette Richards, so he knows about my marriage," she said suddenly.

"If he knows about your marriage, maybe he knows about your divorce, too. Maybe after all this time, he's finally come back for you. Maybe he's come back to make up for the past." Bridget, ever the romantic sighed at the very thought.

Nikki snorted her disbelief, feeling a slight hysteria sweep over her. "Even if he tried, there's no way in hell that man could ever make up for the past," she said with fevered finality.

Greyson Blakemore stood at the window of the second-story room that had been his childhood bedroom. He stared out into the distance where the bright-colored lights of the boardwalk lit the horizon.

Land's End. At one time, he'd thought it was the only place on earth that mattered. It had been his salvation, his sanity.

He opened the window and felt the warm, salt-tinged air caress his face. Wafting on the breeze were the muted musical tones of the carousel's calliope. As if the Pied Piper of Hamelin were using his mythical pipe to summon Grey, the haunting notes pulled at him, beckoned him.

As he stood at the window, with the sounds of the ocean crashing to shore mingling with the distant refrain of the boardwalk, he was thrust backward in time. Like the H.G. Wells's time traveler in his fantasy machine, Grey chose the place and time in his past to revisit.

It was a mental exercise he'd indulged in before, and always when he did, he wound up with Nikki in his arms. She was seventeen and he was eighteen.

He closed his eyes, allowing the past full rein, letting his senses relive that particular moment of yesterday.

Her hair was a long tangle of dark curls that smelled of the sun and held the illumination of the moonlight that shone overhead. He'd held her before, kissed her before, but on this particular night, their embrace held the urgency of summer's end, the knowledge that within two days he would leave for college. On this night, their urgency fed their passion and the passion fed on itself until they reached the point of no return. Even though they had made love a hundred times before, this time was different, already holding the bittersweet pangs of loneliness and separation.

Afterward, he'd stared at her in wonder, as always unable to believe that she was his. Her hazel eyes had taken on the gray hue of the shadows beneath the pier where they lay. Her skin was as warm as the sun-kissed sand. The moonlight caressed her face, emphasizing the straightness of her nose, etching each of her features in stark radiance. At the time, he'd loved her more than anything or anyone on earth. They'd talked of the future, planned their tomorrows...and after that night, he hadn't seen her again...until this evening.

Nikki was as much a part of Grey's past as those youthful carefree summer days. Yet he'd banished her from his very soul. But seeing her again had managed to stir up a strange mixture of emotions that weren't easy to sort out.

"Greyson?"

He turned to see his mother standing in the doorway.

"We're waiting dinner for you."

"I'm sorry. I didn't realize it was so late." He looked at his watch, surprised to see it was after eight o'clock. He smiled apologetically, knowing his mother always had dinner served promptly at eight.

This rigid adherence to customs and habits had been one of the things that had driven him to seek the freedom of the boardwalk so many years ago. There, dinner was whenever you got hungry. The days began in the afternoon and lingered until long into the night. There were no clocks, no schedules, no routines to keep. It was a far different world than the structured environment of his home life.

"Greyson, dear?"

He felt his mother's hand on his sleeve and flushed, realizing his gaze was once again focused out his window. She joined him there, her light, expensive fragrance surrounding him.

"I blame myself, you know," she said, making him turn to look at her curiously. "Your father always said I should have been more firm with you. I should have forbidden you to go to that place."

"I don't think anything you could have said or done would have kept me from the boardwalk." He looked back out the window, seeing the lights of the Ferris wheel, remembering his child's perception of a fantasy kingdom against the darkness of the ocean. "There was a kind of special magic there for me," he said, irritated to recognize a certain wistfulness in his tone.

"But that's all behind you now," his mother said, patting his arm reassuringly. "That was the magic of childhood, but you're a man now with responsibilities.''

Responsibilities . . . yes. For the past seven years, he'd carried much of the responsibilities of the Blakemore family business on his shoulders. And now he held the livelihood of the people at Land's End in the palm of his hands.

He left the window, following his mother. He hesitated at the doorway of the room, catching one last glimpse of the brilliant colored lights reflecting off the ocean waves.

Yes, he'd always thought the boardwalk held some kind of magic. He remembered his youth there with Nikki with a longing that was, at times, physically painful. The bright lights, the gay music, the complete freedom . . . and Nikki. They had all combined to make the past so poignant, so sharply etched in his mind that he was trapped by that very image.

No matter where he'd gone, what he'd done, his thoughts had always drifted back here, to the boardwalk and Nikki. It was an illusion that had made everything else in his life pale by comparison.

Perhaps I needed to come back here, he thought as he followed his mother down the stairs to the dining room. Perhaps in order to finally come to terms with that past, find happiness in the future, he was going to have to dispel the illusion. He wondered if he was going to have to destroy the boardwalk.

Two

Nikki woke slowly, trying to hold on to her dreams, but it was like somebody trying to capture an echo. The sounds of morning intruded on her sleep—the banging of a hammer from someplace outside, the recurrent sloshing of waves acquainting themselves with the shore, Bridget yelling at her Swedish husband, Lars, to take out the garbage.

Dreams of yesterday were chased away, leaving behind a bitter aftertaste in her mouth and the need for a cup of hot coffee.

She stumbled out of bed and pulled on a floor-length silken robe, enjoying the sensual coolness of the material against her naked flesh. Although it was only the beginning of June, it was so unusually hot that Nikki had taken to her youthful penchant for sleeping in the buff.

She belted the robe, then padded into the kitchen and quickly set about making coffee. She frowned as she thought of the dreams that had plagued her sleep all night long. Erotic dreams of Grey... distorted memories of his touch, his caress.

Seeing him again had stirred up embers of the flame that had once burned so brightly inside her. Seeing him again had disrupted the modicum of inner peace she thought she'd finally found.

For seven long years she had worked hard to forget him, to learn to hate him, and now it was more important than ever that she hang on to those negative emotions.

She carried her cup of coffee into the small living room and flopped down on the sofa. Thoughtfully she sipped her coffee as her gaze found the picture on the end table. Johnny. She wondered where he was, what he was doing at this moment. Their marriage had lasted only ten months, but they'd parted as they had begun, as friends. Marrying him had been her second mistake. The first had been falling in love and trusting Grey.

"Hey, Nikki."

"Come on in," Nikki yelled in the direction of the front door, smiling as Bridget stepped inside.

"Good morning," Bridget exclaimed before sailing into the kitchen. She returned a moment later with a cup of coffee cradled between her hands.

Nikki smiled indulgently at her friend. "I thought Lars told you to stay away from caffeine," she commented.

Bridget waved her hands in dismissal. "Oh, him. I think he believes that too much coffee might stunt my growth. I keep telling him it's too late." She grinned like a mischievous child. She took a sip from the mug, then settled back on the sofa. "So, are you ready for the tour today?"

Nikki grimaced. "I've just been sitting here thinking about packing my bags and catching the first train out of town."

"You should have known that as president of the Boardwalk League, you'd be chosen to deal with Grey." She smiled sympathetically. "Honey, we need somebody who's on our side to be with him when he looks over the area. I know it will be difficult, but surely you can be civil to the man, show him around and not jeopardize the future of the boardwalk because of your past."

Nikki nodded wearily. Yes, she knew it was necessary to keep the past firmly buried and focus on the issue at hand—the survival of the boardwalk.

That had to take precedence over her own pain, her own sense of enormous betrayal. The survival of this area had to transcend her own personal torment.

Yesterday at the meeting with the people of the boardwalk, she'd known with a sinking heart that she would be chosen as the one to work with Grey. She'd called him the night before to arrange to give him a tour this morning. No wonder she'd suffered strange dreams about him, she thought suddenly. The dreams had probably been induced by her dread of seeing him yet again, of having to have anything at all to do with him.

"If I'm lucky, he'll take care of the business here, then return to his life in New York City."

"With his father dead, don't you think he'll probably stay here?" Bridget asked.

"I hope not," she replied fervently. But what if he did remain in Oceanview? How was she ever going to cope with seeing him all the time? To survive, she'd have to hang on to her anger and her bitterness. She couldn't afford to think about the stirrings of desire, the passion he'd always evoked in her with a mere glance, a simple touch. Those emotions were dangerous, unwanted...the emotions of a fool.

"Nikki, if he wanted it, couldn't you give him another chance?" Bridget asked gently.

"Never," she replied flatly. "He'll never again have a place in my life. He negated that right when he sent me that envelope full of money for an abortion."

"He was young," Bridget said.

"And so was I," Nikki retorted. "Young and pregnant and alone." Again a deep ache pierced through her, momentarily taking her breath away. "Everyone told me I was a fool, that boardwalk girls had always been easy prey for the town boys. I thought what we had was different...." She shook her head. "I'd be a fool to ever allow Grey to get past my defenses again," she said softly. "And my mama didn't raise no fool." Now, if she could just remember that when she was once again face-to-face with Grey.

Grey walked down the beach toward the huge sign that read: Land's End, The Biggest Little Boardwalk in New Jersey. The boardwalk at Land's End, which stretched for only one mile, couldn't begin to compete with its bigger, more famous seven-mile sister in Atlantic City. However, there was a time when Land's End had been a very popular tourist attraction. Built in the early 1900s, the boardwalk had enjoyed relative success until the last decade.

Grey had heard the stories many times, of how his grandfather had owned the land and had allowed a passing carnival to set up along the board-walk. The carny people had liked the permanency of the place and had worked out a deal to remain there year-round.

It was Grey's father who had parceled out the land and had renters sign leases. All of the original carny people were gone, but some of their descendents were here, along with others who had come seeking someplace to call their very own.

Grey stared up at the huge sign, noting how weathered and faded the lettering had become with the passing of time. He walked beneath it, seeing indications that the boardwalk was beginning to show signs of life. An old man pulled up an awning on one of the concession stands, and a portly woman swept the walkway in front of her darts booth. He looked at his wristwatch. It was just after ten o'clock. In two hours, all the booths and galleries, rides and sideshows would officially open to the public.

In the harsh light of day there was little of the magical-kingdom aura. The sunshine glared off the peeling, faded paint of the buildings. The faint scent of decayed fish and kelp rode the breeze. Even the wood of the boardwalk looked old, cracked by the heat of the sun, buckled with age in many places. He wondered if Nikki, too, would lose her magical aura in the harsh light of the day.

Other than his brief visit two nights ago, it had been seven years since he had been to the boardwalk, but his feet remembered and moved him in the direction of old habits.

He found himself in front of his favorite pizza place, the scent of spicy sauce and warm crust carrying on the salty breeze. The sign in front read: Short Stuff's Pizzeria.

Without conscious thought he moved around the side of the building to the back door. When he opened it, the door creaked just as it used to. Smiling in memory, he stepped into the dimness of the back room. The place wasn't empty. There were about eight kids sitting at an old picnic table, eating from a platter of pizza that sat in the middle of the table. Some things never change, he thought.

For a moment, he felt as if he'd stepped backward in time. He sat down at a small table near where the kids sat and allowed the ambience to overtake him.

This is where he'd come every day for lunch, to see Nikki and eat his fill of Bridget's "mistakes." He closed his eyes, remembering the anticipation that each afternoon he'd run across the hot sand of the beach to come here, eager to see Nikki, hold her in his arms, steal a kiss from her in the small kitchen of the restaurant. He'd grab her by the waist and pull her up against him, unashamed of his aching desire for her. Those kisses . . . she tasted of pepperoni and tomato sauce, and her hair smelled of doughy crust.

"Hmm, you taste so good," he'd whisper in her ear, then he'd lean down to explore her lips again.

"You taste better." She would laugh, and with the tip of her tongue she would trace the contours of his mouth while she teasingly pressed her body intimately against his.

She'd loved to tease him, but he hadn't minded. He'd known instinctively that the promises she made with her eyes and caresses would eventually be fulfilled. He'd never doubted that at night, when the shadows deepened beneath the boardwalk, they'd meet and follow through on the teasing promises they'd made to each other during the light of day.

He forced his attention back to the present, and realized that coming here had been a mistake. The scent of the pizza, the kid's laughter, the warmth of the room, all combined to bring back memories Grey didn't want to entertain.

He could still remember his rage when two months after he'd gone to college, his father had brought the news clipping announcing her wedding. Grey had fallen apart, and he now realized that even after all this time, he still hadn't completely pulled himself together.

Yes, this was a mistake, coming to this pizza place where the memories were as pungent as the scent of garlic and oregano. He stood up to leave, and at that moment Nikki entered the room from the kitchen, carrying a platter of pizza slices.

She saw him immediately and for a moment she froze, like a frightened deer caught in the brilliant beams of a car's headlight. He saw the color rise in her cheeks, saw her large hazel eyes darken in some indefinable emotion and he wondered if she remembered those summer days when Bridget's kitchen had served as one of their trysting places where they had both learned about the hypnotic power of love and sex. He felt a heaviness begin in his loins, the stirrings of a desire he now found repugnant.

Memories slammed into Nikki's head, memories she had repressed for a very long time.

"Hurry Grey, kiss me before Bridget comes back in."

"I don't want to kiss you in a hurry. I want to kiss you slowly, thoroughly." She'd giggled, but raised her lips once again, seeking the heat of his.

"Tonight," she'd promised, arching her back as his hands pressed her lower body closer against him.

"Nikki, don't move like that against me or I can't be held responsible for my actions."

"I like it when you aren't responsible for your actions."

His eyes had been dark and dangerous and she had loved it, loved him.

Even now, she felt her breasts responding to the vividness of her memories, her nipples tightening and surging against her T-shirt. She jerked her gaze away from him, appalled at her body's traitorous weakness, her mind's lapse of sanity.

"Here we are, kids," she said, forcing a light-hearted tone as she set the pizza on the table. She was conscious of Grey's gaze still on her. She steeled herself against the onslaught of emotions and walked over to where he sat at the small table.

"I thought we were meeting at the theater in an hour," she said.

"I just wanted to see if Bridget still ran her soup kitchen for the kids."

"Every day, although you know she'd kick you in the shin if she heard you refer to it as a soup kitchen. Bridget maintains she's merely getting rid of all the 'mistakes' she can't serve to paying customers."

Grey nodded, a ghost of a smile moving a corner of his mouth. "If Bridget really made as many mistakes as she says she does, she'd have been out of business a long time ago."

"You know Bridget feeds a lot of hungry children...some of whom won't get another meal until tomorrow morning when they return here." Nikki leaned forward, focusing on the issue at hand

and trying to ignore the way his familiar scent surrounded her. "Grey, these kids come from broken homes, they have alcoholic or drug-dependent parents. Bridget not only gives them a hot meal, she also gives them a sympathetic ear, friendly support, a reason to go on fighting to make something of themselves."

"Nikki, you don't have to convince me about the good Bridget does here. Have you forgotten that I was one of Bridget's waifs?"

She straightened her shoulders defensively. "No, I haven't forgotten that. I just want to make sure *you* haven't. The people on the boardwalk were good to you. They didn't care who your family was or what your problems were. They accepted you without reservation."

"That's true," he agreed, his tone suddenly weary.

"Then how can you think of closing us down?" she asked with a touch of anger.

"Nikki, I can't make a business decision based on the fact that some people were nice to me years ago. I have to make a decision based on my head, not my heart."

At that moment, Bridget entered from the kitchen. "What's this? A new boy on the boardwalk?" Her face beamed a smile as she approached Grey and Nikki. "Greyson Blake-more . . . all grown-up and looking mighty fine."

"Hello, Bridget, you're looking ravishing your-self," Grey said, returning a smile to the little woman who immediately joined him at the table.

"I heard you were back. It's about time you re-turned to your roots. What kept you away for so long?" Bridget asked.

Grey shrugged, his answer lost as Nikki fled into the kitchen. Once there, she leaned against the stainless steel refrigerator door, remembering his arms wrapped around her, the two of them lying in the sand. "Forever," he'd whispered in her ear and she'd believed him. Damn him for his lies. Damn him for making her think their love could over-come the differences in their backgrounds . . . anything the world threw at them. Damn him for making forever so very brief.

"Nikki?" Bridget entered the kitchen. "Grey says he's ready for his tour whenever you are. He'll wait for you outside."

Nikki sighed. "I might as well get it over with," she said more to herself than to Bridget. After tak-ing a deep breath, she walked through the back room and out into the sunshine. "Where to first?" she asked without preamble.

He pulled a handful of papers out of his pocket. "Before he died, my father had been receiving complaints about safety violations. I thought we'd check those out first.''

''I can't imagine what kind of violations there would be concerning safety. Sure, things need painting, but safety has always been a priority here.''

He handed her one of the papers, a letter written complaining about the hazardous condition of the Ferris wheel. She scanned the contents quickly. ''You can't take this seriously,'' she scoffed. ''Whoever sent it didn't even sign it. Probably one of the townspeople who didn't win a stuffed animal and wrote this in a snit.''

''Still, I intend to take it seriously,'' he returned evenly. ''Nikki, if there's any chance of keeping the boardwalk open, I'm going to have to see what kinds of obstacles we're facing, what kind of financial backing it will take to make Land's End more profitable. So, we take these things one at a time and check them out, okay?''

Minutes later as Pete Ely, the Ferris wheel owner, showed Grey the documentation of recent safety inspections, Nikki studied Grey, trying to attain some objectivity. It had been easier to maintain distance when she'd seen him before, when he'd been dressed in his tailored suit and expensive dress shirt. But today, wearing a pair of worn dungarees and a short-sleeved sports shirt, he was uncomfortably like the Grey of her youth, the Grey she had loved with a passion that had been all-ending.

But the man of her past had made his choices. He chose to end his responsibility to her with an envelope of money. Blakemores didn't get involved with boardwalk brats—how many times had she been warned of that? Still, she'd been certain in her heart that Grey wasn't like the other Blakemores. She'd been wrong.

She wished he'd married. Perhaps if he was married, she wouldn't be feeling the insidious stirrings of temptation. Every time she looked into the dark depths of his eyes, she saw an image of a serpent, whispering that it was safe to taste the juicy apple. But she'd already tasted the meat of the fruit, and she'd discovered that it bore bitter seeds.

"Well, I guess this takes care of that particular issue," Grey said, frowning as he looked up at the Ferris wheel. "Although it certainly could use a fresh coat of paint."

"Everything around here could use a fresh coat of paint," Nikki replied. "We went to your father several months ago and asked if he would be willing to lower the rent for a few months so we could use the extra money to make some improvements, but he refused."

"Point taken," he replied as he moved in the direction of the carousel. Nikki lagged behind, dreading to go to the place where it had all begun so many years ago.

His footsteps slowed as he approached the ancient merry-go-round and she wondered if he, too, was entertaining thoughts from the past.

She watched as he stepped up on the carousel's platform, his feet moving him toward the huge silver steed they'd fought over. He placed a hand on the saddle that had once been such a brilliant blue, but was now worn to the paleness of distant dreams. "It hardly seems worth fighting over now, does it?" He smiled wistfully and ran his hand lightly down the horse's flank. "In my mind, it was always bigger, brighter."

"I guess when you look back, you always remember things as being much better than they really were," she said pointedly.

"Who's running the equipment now?" he asked, removing his hand from the horse as dark shutters slid into place over his eyes.

"Walt Simon."

"Walt Simon? He must be a hundred years old by now."

Nikki couldn't hide a small smile. Everyone was surprised by Walt's longevity and eternally youthful spirit. At that moment, Walt himself walked out from behind the ticket booth, his keen blue eyes immediately spying Nikki and Grey.

"Well, I'll be damned," he exclaimed, moving toward them with the peculiar gait of age and arthritis. He held out his hand to Grey, who clasped it and shook it vigorously. "Well, I'll be double-damned." He grinned, a toothless smile that transformed his grizzled, weathered face into that of an innocent child. "I knew you wouldn't stay away forever. You and Nikki were my very best customers for a lot of summers. First ones on when I opened and the last ones to ride before I'd close up. Remember?"

"I remember," Grey said, smiling tightly as he dropped the old man's hand.

"Yes, sir," Walt said with a wistful smile that fully displayed his toothless gums. "Those were the days. The walkways were filled with people, and I'd have lines of kiddies waiting to ride the fellas." Walt frowned suddenly. "I don't get lines anymore." He looked at Grey anxiously. "Have you come back to help us? Have you come to breathe life back into Land's End?"

"He doesn't know whether to breathe life into it or suck the last of its life out of it," Nikki explained.

"Suck the...you mean close us down?" Walt looked at Grey incredulously. "But, you wouldn't do that, would you, Grey?"

Grey grimaced. "Walt, I'm trying to make a sound business decision."

"Grey has taken over the Blakemore family business interests," Nikki interjected.

"But you never were like the rest of those people," Walt protested. "Your family always made business decisions, but you always made heart decisions." He gazed at Grey in sadness. "I don't understand nothing anymore." He ran a gnarled hand through his thin, gray hair. "I've fought the Blakemores for the past fifty years. I always thought you'd be different . . . somehow better."

Nikki noted the slight flush of color that suffused Grey's face as he stiffened his back. "There's nothing to understand, Walt. I have obligations and priorities. I am a Blakemore."

And don't ever forget it, Nikki mentally added. There was a time when she had forgotten, but she had paid the price and now would never make that mistake again.

"You know, if you decide to close us down and move us off, we won't make it easy for you," Walt observed. He grinned like a mischievous boy. "Me and the fellas—" he gestured to the carousel horses "—we can be pretty damn stubborn when we set our minds to it."

Grey's eyes glinted with a touch of admiration at Walt's distinct challenge.

From the carousel they moved on, Grey surveying the condition of the wooden walkways, making notes about everything he saw.

Nikki found herself seeing the area through his eyes, and what she saw made her despair. So much was required, so much needed to be done. Nobody wanted to come to a tourist area that smelled of hopelessness.

What they needed was somebody who cared, somebody who would risk making an investment in the area. Grey's father, Thomas Blakemore, hadn't cared. He'd only wanted to collect the rent money due him each month.

Did Grey care? She didn't know anymore. She didn't know *him* anymore. He'd once cared deeply, passionately for this area and its people. She watched him as he studied Jim's guns at the shooting gallery. Could she somehow tap into those old feelings he'd once had for the boardwalk? For the sake of her friends, she hoped so. But she wasn't sure if it was possible. After all, he'd also once cared deeply and passionately for her, but that feeling had died a swift and permanent death.

"I don't know, Nikki," he said moments later as he moved to where she stood looking out over the water. "It doesn't look good." He carefully folded the notes he'd made and placed them into his pocket, knowing he'd spend half the night viewing and reviewing, analyzing and reanalyzing his observations. "I see a lot on the minus side of the balance sheet and not many pluses."

"There's one thing you won't find written down on your reports…the enchantment. Grey, have you forgotten the enchantment of Land's End? Have you forgotten how this place embraced you, captivated you, make you feel welcome and safe?"

Unconsciously, she reached out and grabbed his forearm. "Grey, you used to say there was magic here. It's still here, it's just become tarnished with age, smeared by too much wear and too little care." She released her hold on him and moved away, the breeze moving her long hair back from her features, the sun creating fires in the dark strands. "We have dreams, Grey. All of us here on the boardwalk, and you hold them in your hands."

He watched her with narrowed eyes, trying not to see the way the gentle wind molded her T-shirt against her firm, upthrust breasts, trying not to notice the length of her tanned, shapely legs beneath her shorts.

"Dreams are for kids," he replied brusquely, tearing his gaze away from her and back to the water.

"That's not true," she protested. "Dreams are for everyone who has hope, including those here at Land's End that don't have money, or have physical handicaps or whatever. The one commodity they have in abundance is hope." She reached out to grab his arm. "Grey, please don't take that hope away from us. Give us a chance to tell you our dreams before you make the decision to destroy this place.''

Grey ran his hand through his hair, needing to think, but not knowing what to think. Her words reminded him of what this place had once meant to him. He moved away from her, again looking out to the water as if the answers were all there in the waves.

He also realized something else. Despite the fact that she'd betrayed him, married another and gone on with her life, he still wanted her. He wanted her with a passion that was mindless, careless and insane.

What he didn't know was if this, too, was merely a lingering emotion from the past, a memory too powerful to dispel. Would making love to her now be the overwhelming experience he remembered it to be, or had he colored their union with sensations intensified through the haze of time?

The memory was a strange kind of thing, easily given to exaggeration and glorification. Grey had made love with other women since Nikki, but never had he reached the same feeling of completeness he had with her. Had that merely been an illusion?

''Grey?''

''All right,'' he said, suddenly knowing what he wanted. He gazed at her, wanting to fall into the shadows of her eyes, wanting to replay the past, make their ending different this time. ''If you want me to save the boardwalk, you have to show me the magic again.''

She stared at him and he could see the tumultuous emotions in her eyes. Like storm clouds in an early spring sky, they rolled and thundered, but beneath their turbulence, he saw something else, a spark of desire that flamed momentarily, then was quickly doused. She raised her chin and eyed him proudly and he was reminded once again of that first time he'd seen her. Looking back, he wondered if it wasn't then, that very first time, that he'd fallen in love with her.

She'd been so alien, so exotic-looking compared to the other girls he knew from school. She'd been barefoot, her legs sporting a deep tan that didn't quite cover the bruised kneecaps and skinned shins.

She looked like a homeless waif, and yet there was the glory of freedom in her eyes, a self-awareness that he found fascinating. She was like an entity from another planet and he wanted to possess her, contain her spirit and learn from it.

He felt the same way now, as he waited for her answer.

She tossed her hair away from her face and looked at him, her eyes glittering with challenge. ''Okay, Grey, I'll show you the magic,'' she finally answered.

Unconsciously, he took a step toward her, over-come with the need to take her in his arms, feel her body pressed tightly against his.

Her eyes flared slightly as if she read his intent and she took a step back from him. "I've got to get to the theater," she said as she looked at her watch. With a stiff nod, she turned and fled.

He watched her go, wishing he could call back yesterday, wondering exactly what had gone wrong between them, knowing that it wasn't over yet. He knew in that instant that he couldn't go ahead with his future until he resolved this issue from his past. He needed one more night of holding her in his arms. He needed just one more night under the boardwalk with her. Then, just maybe, he could finally let her go.

Three

——

"**I** can't believe I actually agreed," Nikki said the next morning as she poured Bridget a cup of coffee. "Show me the magic, he says, and I say okay. I should have my head examined."

Bridget reached out and patted Nikki's arm in consolation. "But if you can show it to him, maybe he'll save the boardwalk."

"I don't even know if it's possible. Either you see magic or you don't. It has to exist in your soul before you can see it in the world around you—" She broke off in frustration.

She got up from the table and walked over to the window and peered out into the early morning sunshine. ''When a magician pulls a card out of thin air, some people see a man good at sleight of hand, hear a telltale rustle of clothing, notice a furtive grab up a sleeve. Others see only the magic. Grey used to see it, but he's had seven years to perfect the Blakemore skepticism and disbelief. How can I make him see the magic? What can I possibly do to change his mind about the boardwalk? This whole idea is completely ridiculous.'' Nikki sat down at the table and looked at her friend.

Bridget calmly stirred three spoonfuls of sugar into her coffee, a smile wrinkling her perky nose. ''I can't think of anyone more suited to remind Grey of what this boardwalk once was, what it could be again. There is magic here, the magic of wounded people coming together in tolerance, living together in peace, working together and sharing their dreams.''

She reached across the table and grabbed Nikki's hand in hers. ''This boardwalk has given to you all these years. When you were sixteen and your mother died, these people rallied around to make certain you didn't end up in social services. We're a family here, and this family is depending on you, Nikki. You must do *whatever* it takes to make Grey see the magic. You have to do whatever must be done to see that he doesn't close us down...even if it means forgiving him.''

"Never," Nikki replied flatly, removing her hand from Bridget's grasp. "I'll be civil to him, I'll do anything else it takes, but I can never, ever forgive him.''

Bridget paused a moment to take a sip of her coffee, her bright eyes studying Nikki over the top of her cup. "You'll never really be whole again until you get rid of your bitterness," she observed. "Your anger will keep you forever bound to Grey. You need to talk to him, vent it, forgive him. That's the only way you can get on with the rest of your life.''

Bridget's words played and replayed through Nikki's mind for the rest of the morning. Talk to Grey about the past? Ridiculous. The time for talking had long passed. Forgive him? Impossible. Her anger was what kept her strong. Her bitterness was what kept the grief at bay...grief she'd never fully acknowledged, refused to give in to, fearing it would destroy her.

Still, she knew Bridget was right about one thing. The boardwalk and its people had been good to her, had nurtured her. She'd always felt safe here. This was her home, the people were her family, and she owed them a lot.

Somehow, Grey had placed the weight of saving the boardwalk on her head, and she knew for the sake of the people she loved, she had to rise to the challenge.

The morning sunshine was warm as she carried her box of supplies out onto the front porch and set to work crafting a new marionette to add to her act. She smiled as she pulled out her half-completed new puppet. It was a fat, white rat. The kids would love it. At the moment, it was faceless and she hoped to finish it in the next day or two and incorporate it into the show.

As she worked on the marionette, a tenuous sense of contentment swept through her. These were her children, the puppets she fashioned from wood and cloth. These were the children she dressed in ruffles and bows, little baseball caps and suspenders.

Because of the complications of Lolly's stillbirth, the doctor had told Nikki she probably wouldn't be able to get pregnant again. So, she knew these puppets were probably the only children she would ever have, and she fashioned each and every one with love. She closed her eyes for a moment, fighting away the deep grief that always accompanied these thoughts. No babies to hold, no children to love, only emptiness.... She shook her head and refocused on her puppets.

She worked until nearly noon, then packed everything away and headed for the theater. The sun was brilliant overhead and already she could feel the heat of the baked walkway through the thin soles of her sandals.

She was grateful that she'd finally been able to afford an air-conditioning unit for the small puppet theater. Hopefully, the promise of a half-hour respite in the cool darkness would entice the tourists to enter and enjoy her productions.

She unlocked the door and stepped inside, immediately flipping on a light against the complete darkness of the interior.

"You haven't changed the locks." Grey's deep voice greeted her, causing her to squeal and jump around in surprise.

He sat in the front row, his long, lean frame looking ridiculous in the small chairs that usually accommodated giggling children. But he couldn't be mistaken for a child. His entire body radiated raw masculinity and a potent sexuality he'd always been oblivious to possessing.

"How...did you get in?" she asked, irritated by the sudden erratic thudding of her heart. His unexpected appearance had just scared her, she rationalized, refusing to believe that her rapid heartbeat had anything to do with the burst of electricity the air seemed to contain.

He held up a key—the one she had given him years ago, when the two of them had often met here to be alone. She hated him for reminding her of those times, hated him for feeling as if he still had the right to use that key.

"What...what are you doing here?" she asked. Before giving him a chance to answer, she went around behind the backdrop curtain of the stage, as if the dark drapery would provide a shield against his powerful presence.

"I thought it might be a good idea if you called a meeting so I can hear some of the ideas everyone on the boardwalk has for the area's rejuvenation."

"I think that's a wonderful idea," she immediately agreed. "We tried to get your father to come to a meeting and see what sorts of compromises could be reached, but he wasn't interested." Besides, she mentally added, the sooner they resolved the issue of the boardwalk, hopefully the sooner Grey would find other business to occupy him and keep him far away from the boardwalk and her.

"I am not my father." His voice came from right next to her in the confines of the backstage area.

"You may find it difficult to convince the people here that you don't have the same priorities as your father...profit first, everything else second." She tensed, feeling trapped in the small area with him standing so near.

"And what do you think?" He took a step closer to her, bringing with him a wave of spicy cologne and an evocative body heat that played havoc with her senses. A wave of answering heat swept through her. It was completely unwanted but impossible to tamp down.

"It doesn't matter what I think," she replied. She busied herself with the puppets hanging on hooks against the wall, wishing he would just go away, wishing he'd never come back. Damn Thomas Blakemore for dying and leaving Grey in charge. "Was there anything else?" she asked, hoping he couldn't hear the strain in her voice.

"I'd like to see the area when it's the busiest. What time is the biggest crowd here?"

She refused to look at him. She took a step backward, finding his proximity uncomfortable. "Usually around nine at night."

"I'd like you to be with me when I look around. You promised to show me the magic, Nikki." His voice was soft, like a whispered memory in the back of her brain.

She stiffened against it, once more regretting her impulsive assent to his ridiculous challenge. She must have been out of her mind when she'd promised something so absurd.

Still, she'd never backed away from anything or anyone. Taking a deep breath, she looked at him. "Why don't we meet here at nine tonight?"

He frowned. "I'll need to be home tonight. My mother is giving one of her soirees and insists I be there. What about tomorrow night?"

"Fine," she answered succinctly. "I've got to get ready for the first show," she finally said when he made no move to leave. She looked at him, noting how the gray shirt he wore perfectly matched the gunmetal shade of his eyes. He had bedroom eyes, with dark thick lashes framing the gray depths.

Before she could guess his intent, he reached out and placed a hand on her shoulder, the heat piercing her T-shirt to saturate the skin beneath. "Nikki, I think we need to talk about what went wrong, what happened between us."

She twisted away from him. "Well, I don't," she replied unevenly, her heart resuming its frantic pound. "It's dead, Grey. The past is dead and buried and nothing is served by talking about it. It was youth and immaturity and nothing more." She drew in a deep breath to steady the trembling that had suffused her body at his mere touch. "Just leave it alone, Grey. It's done. It's over and no amount of talking can change anything."

For a long moment, he searched her face, as if weighing the option of pushing the issue with her. Finally, he nodded. "Then I'll see you tomorrow night," he replied.

He turned and left, and Nikki expelled a breath of relief. The backstage area that had seemed to shrink in an effort to contain his presence, shifted back to its normal size.

Nikki checked to make certain everything backstage was ready for the day's performances, then grabbed a broom and went up front. As she swept the previous day's sand and grit out the front door, her thoughts returned to Grey.

He should have come back fat and bald. He should have come back dissipated from too much alcohol, or unhappily married to a shallow society twit. It wasn't fair that he had returned and still had the power to make her knees weak and her head spin. It wasn't fair that he made her remember what they'd had . . . and what had been destroyed.

He'd wanted to talk about what had happened . . . as if any amount of discussion could somehow rectify the past. She tightened her grip on the broom handle, moving briskly across the tiled floor. She didn't want to talk about the past. There was simply nothing to discuss. She'd finally learned to live with the tragedy of Grey's betrayal and her daughter's death. She'd come to terms with the fact that there would never be any more children for her.

She leaned against the wall and drew in a deep breath. What she couldn't understand was why . . . why after living through the pain and hell of Grey once, did she now feel an overwhelming urge to once again melt into his arms and know the splendor of his embrace?

Why was there a small part of her that held tight to the beautiful memory and the wonder of what had once been between them? And why, dear heaven, was there a fragment of her heart that wanted it again?

Nikki wound her way down the overgrown path that led to the Land's End Cemetery. The fingers of twilight painted the area in lush gold and pink tones and cast long shadows that danced on the ground with every step she took. The only sounds were the soft calls of birds and the whisper of the grass as she walked.

It had been a while since she had come here. When the hour break she had for dinner had arrived, she realized it was time for another visit. She needed to come.

She also needed to find time to get out here and mow, she observed as the tall grass tickled her ankles. Unlike the cemetery in Oceanview that had a lawn maintenance service to take care of the grounds, the cemetery for the boardwalk people depended on friends and relatives for upkeep.

She walked past the older headstones, the ones marking the resting place for many of the very first carny people. There were no flowers on any of the graves. The boardwalk people believed in celebrating life, loving people while they were alive, not memorializing them after death.

She moved past newer headstones bearing the names of people she had known in childhood.

Nikki's mother was here, nestled beneath the shade of a tree. She paused only a moment there, her heart whispering a greeting of love. But it wasn't this grave that called to her. It was another.

She finally stopped by a tiny grave with a headstone bearing the image of a little cherub angel with wings. The stone read simply: Lolly Richards.

As Nikki stood staring down at the small grave, her heart ached with the peculiar edge of emptiness that was at once familiar and devastating. Funny, she'd thought some of the pain would be gone by now. Each time she visited her child's grave, she expected the sharp jab of heartache to be lessened, but it was always there just as violent and breath-stealing as ever.

In the first year after Lolly's stillbirth, she'd lived with the pain of loss every single day. She would awaken with it in the morning and go to sleep with it at night. At first, she had come here every weekend to grieve, but through the last year, she had limited her trips, trying to gain control of the constant pain.

She thought it had worked, but as she crouched to sit in the lush grass, she felt the sting of tears burning her eyes and knew the grief she felt for her child would never end.

"Oh, Lolly," she murmured. She'd loved the child while she was in her womb, but had never had the chance to love her once she was born. After forty hours of horrible labor and complications, Lolly was dead.

A sob caught in her throat as she remembered the doctor placing the baby in her arms to allow her a final goodbye. She'd been cleaned up and wrapped in a pale pink blanket. She'd been perfect...ten fingers and ten toes, delicate little features that were a blend of mother and father...feathery dark hair the same darkness as Grey's, a full mouth in the image of Nikki's. Nikki had traced the contours of the tiny face, kissed the pale forehead with lingering love and said goodbye to her little girl.

She shook herself, shoving those memories into the place where she rarely went to retrieve them. She began to weed around the headstone, hoping the physical activity would ease the burden of her tears.

Lolly Richards. The stone should have read Lolly Blakemore. When Nikki had discovered she was pregnant, she'd immediately written Grey at college, certain that he would be happy, that they would get married. She'd received an envelope of money, no note, no explanation in return. She'd been destroyed.

Nikki had entertained the idea of an abortion, but realized she couldn't follow through on it. The baby inside her was the only piece of Grey she would have forever.

Still, the thought of having the baby alone was daunting. She had been seventeen years old, scared to death and completely alone.

Johnny Richards had been one of the drifters the boardwalk lured. An attractive, charming man who'd instantly struck up a friendship with Nikki. When he'd offered to marry her to give the baby a name, she'd agreed.

It had been a decision based on need, on fear. Soon after Lolly's stillbirth, she and Johnny had decided to divorce, both knowing their marriage had been an impetuous decision.

Johnny had drifted off into the sunset, and she had never seen him again, although she occasionally received letters from him telling her of his travels.

Nikki breathed a tremulous sigh and stood up. She'd been foolish to come here and stir up old memories. She only managed to renew the pain she fought against every day.

All she needed to take away with her from here was the thundering anger at Grey's betrayal. The anger was positive...a good thing for her to hug close to her. The anger was her only defense against Grey and evocative memories of youth and love.

"I won't forget," she said aloud. "I can't ever forgive him," she added, then turned and walked away.

* * *

Grey walked out the back door and onto the Blakemore terrace, breathing deeply of the warm, salt-tinged air. It was a welcome respite from the smells of rich food and expensive perfume that permeated the inside of the house.

He sat down on one of the wrought-iron patio chairs and rubbed his forehead, where a headache had begun simultaneously with the arrival of his mother's first guests.

The carnival sounds of the boardwalk floated on the breeze and battled with the party noise that drifted out of the house. He sighed, knowing the party inside would last long into the night. There was nothing his mother's friends loved more than an opportunity to drink cocktails, eat fancy hors d'oeuvres and gossip about those who'd not been able to attend.

He glanced out into the distance. From this vantage point, only the very top of the Ferris wheel was visible, its lights creating a glow of gaiety against the backdrop of the night sky. And somehow, the brilliant illumination brought Nikki to his mind.

He looked at his watch. Seven o'clock. She would be at the theater for the evening performances. Funny, he'd thought he'd moved beyond her, outgrown her. When he'd learned of her marriage, he'd immersed himself first in college, then in the New York interests of the Blakemore business.

He'd made a life for himself that many envied. He ate at the finest restaurants, escorted New York City's most beautiful, prominent women to the theater and to charity benefits.

Yet always there had been a part of him that had longed for the simplicity of the boardwalk, that had ached for the glory he'd found in Nikki's embrace. Always there had been a deep ache within that nothing seemed to assuage.

Had the magic between them simply been the idealism of youth as she had said? Had youth been responsible for that feeling of belonging he'd always found in her arms? Was it a fleeting thing only experienced once in a lifetime, then forever gone? Somehow, it didn't seem fair to waste the intensity of emotion on the young.

"Oh, here you are," a feminine voice said from behind him.

He tensed slightly, then turned and smiled at Amanda Barrington. She sat down on the chair next to him, her pungent perfume intensifying his headache.

"I wondered where you'd gotten to," she said, crossing her legs to give him the best view of her shapely thighs.

"I just thought I'd get a breath of fresh air," he answered. He knew Amanda had been invited in a feeble attempt by his mother to play matchmaker.

Amanda came from the "right" background and had the "right" upbringing.

He rubbed his forehead, trying to force out the instant mental vision he got of Nikki, splendid and naked, unashamed and free, running on the sand as moonlight reflected off her body. Amanda would never run naked on a moonlit beach.

"Headache?" Amanda asked, her voice a practiced purr of sympathy.

"A little one," he admitted.

"Here, let me." She moved to stand directly behind him and placed her fingertips on his forehead. Her fingers were cold, bloodless. As she massaged, she leaned into him, pressing her small breasts seductively against his back. They felt hard and unappealing . . . like Amanda herself.

"Thanks, that's much better," he said after a moment. He stood up and smiled in forced pleasantness. "Shall we go join the others?"

A fleeting disappointment pinched her features but was quickly replaced with a smooth, studied smile. She linked her arm through his and together they returned to the crowd and noise inside.

Grey lasted another two hours, then escaped unnoticed to the quiet confines of his room. Once there, his gaze was drawn out the window, toward the colorful lights of the boardwalk.

He knew his mother would wonder where he'd disappeared to, but the party had become intolerable and he couldn't stand it another minute. Amanda and her superficial conversation and cloying perfume, the affluent people who spoke in rhymes, never saying what they meant, never meaning what they said...all had combined to make him feel suffocated.

Almost unconsciously, he swept off his suit jacket and yanked impatiently at his tie. He stepped out of his slacks and fumbled with the buttons of his shirt, suddenly needing to be out of the stifling formal clothing.

He rummaged around in a bottom drawer full of old clothes until he found a worn T-shirt and a pair of cutoff denim shorts.

Redressed, he sneaked down the back stairway and into the kitchen, grateful that the room was momentarily empty. It wasn't until he was out the back door and running on the beach that he realized his intent.

He headed toward the boardwalk to find Nikki. He wanted to discover if the magic that had once existed between them had been real, or if it had been manufactured by wistful youth and the first blossoms of sexual awakening? It suddenly seemed vital that he know if what he and Nikki had shared was real, or a mirage painted glossy by distance and time?

Four

The night air embraced Grey as he jogged across the sandy beach. It invigorated him, being out of the confines of his house. With warm, humid fingers, the breeze stroked his skin with its familiar scent of the ocean waves. The moonlight couldn't compete with the brilliance of the colored lights that flickered and danced on the wires in the light wind off the water.

He should have come back years ago, he thought as he ran. He'd missed the boardwalk and all the freedom it had afforded him. He'd missed the salty air, the scent of excitement and roasting hot dogs, and Nikki.

He should have returned and faced her when he'd heard about her divorce. It had been his own pride that had kept him away. After all, he'd been at college only a couple of months when she'd chosen to marry another man.

Had she fallen desperately, hopelessly in love? For some reason, this thought brought a shaft of deep, rich pain rushing through him. He'd once believed she'd been desperately, hopelessly in love with *him*.

Over the years, in moments of solitude, he'd often gone back in his mind and tried to figure out exactly what had happened between them, but there weren't any concrete answers.

She'd been the open book in his life, the unfinished business. She had been the one without closure, and he wondered vaguely if that's what had brought him back to the boardwalk, the need to finally close the book on Nikki and those distant, haunting visions of passion past but not forgotten.

He slowed his pace when his feet hit the first board of the walkway. Around him life surged, snapping electrically in the air, vibrating the wood beneath his feet. From the direction of the roller coaster came screams, while the kiddies' rides produced the sounds of childish giggling and gaiety.

A burst of abandoned laughter rose to his lips, the sound surprising him. How long had it been since he had fully expressed any genuine joy? Too long. There had been a time when laughter had come easily, but that particular sound had been stifled beneath the drudgery of too many work hours and too many board meetings. God, he'd missed this place.

It was strange the curveballs life threw. He'd never particularly wanted to be a part of Blakemore Enterprises, but once Nikki had married, he'd been adrift and his father had quickly capitalized on Grey's confusion. Upon graduation, he'd found himself in charge of the New York companies while his father had continued to run the boardwalk interests. In death, Thomas Blakemore had unwittingly given his son what he wanted, a reason to return to the boardwalk.

Shoving aside these thoughts, he headed for the theater, stopping only long enough to buy some cotton candy. As he walked down the noisy walkway, eating the sugary confection, a sense of quiet contentment drifted through him. There was nothing like cotton candy to make the worries and problems of the world fade away. He grinned at his own absurdity.

He was disappointed when he got to the puppet theater and found it closed for the night. He looked at his watch and sighed. Of course, it was nearly ten o'clock and she had told him earlier that her last performance was over at nine.

He frowned, wondering where to go from here. She could be anywhere—up high in a seat on the Ferris wheel, or winding through the maze in the house of mirrors. However, he knew his best bet would be Bridget's pizza place. In their youth, they'd often ended their evenings at Bridget's.

He walked in that direction, his head filled with the sights and sounds surrounding him. It was easy to feel completely free here. There was a curious sense of anonymity, a wildness in the air that made anything seem possible.

Bridget's place was packed. He made his way through the tables, smiling and waving at several people he recognized from town. He pushed against the swinging door and entered the kitchen.

Bridget stood at the counter, the front of her covered with flour as she twirled a pizza crust into shape. "Well, look what the cat dragged in." Bridget's eyes twinkled merrily as she grinned at him. "You here to eat, or what?"

He shook his head. "Actually, I was wondering if Nikki was around."

"Not tonight. She went back to her place right after her last show."

"Thanks. She live in the same house?"

Bridget nodded.

Grey turned to leave, but hesitated when Bridget called after him. He turned around to face her.

"You know, I love that girl...love her like she was my own daughter. She's fragile now and she's had enough hurt to last her a lifetime. Don't you be adding to it."

"I don't intend to," he answered in surprise.

Once he was back outside, he paused a moment and leaned against the wooden railing that faced the ocean.

It was difficult to think of Nikki as fragile. She'd always been so headstrong, so sure of herself. She'd possessed a daunting self-confidence that he'd envied, a touch of arrogance he'd always found appealing.

Suddenly, for the first time since returning to Oceanview and Land's End, Grey realized that the girl he'd loved seven years ago may no longer exist.

She'd experienced seven years of life he hadn't been a part of, knew nothing about. The Nikki of his past might well be gone forever, and the Nikki of the present a complete stranger.

He didn't think he had changed much at all with the passing of time. He'd dated, but nobody special. He'd worked hard, but at times wondered if he'd accomplished anything worthwhile. He smiled slightly, ruefully. And after all this time, he was still running to the boardwalk to escape his mother's parties.

Bridget had nothing to worry about. He had no intention of hurting Nikki, he thought as he walked the short distance to her cottage. He wasn't sure what he wanted from her. He just knew that somehow it wasn't finished, and Grey never left anything unfinished.

A few minutes later, he stood in front of her house. It looked much the same as it had years before. Weathered and needing a fresh coat of paint, it also had a front porch that slanted noticeably to one side.

He'd spent a lot of time here, first when her mother had been alive, then when Bridget had moved in with her. He wondered if the screen on her bedroom window was still missing.

She answered the door on his second knock, obviously surprised by his presence. "Grey." Her eyes widened and she pulled the silk robe closer around her, but not before he caught a glimpse of a tanned collarbone and a flash of long golden legs. "What...what are you doing here?"

He shrugged. He'd thought he'd had an idea, but seeing the guarded expression in her eyes, the vulnerability that trembled one corner of her mouth, he wasn't so sure now. "I found myself free and thought you'd take me around the boardwalk, point out what changes have occurred since I've been gone,'' he finally said.

"But don't you have another commitment... your mother's party?"

"I thought that I'd grown up enough to enjoy them, but I was wrong. It was boring and stiff. I sneaked out at the first opportunity." He smiled, hoping to coax an answering one from her. It didn't work. She remained intensely sober, her gaze not quite meeting his. "Look." He sighed. "This was probably a bad idea. It was just an impulse on my part. We can make it tomorrow night as we'd planned."

"No, it's all right. Uh, come on in. It will just take me a few minutes to get dressed." She opened the door for him and he stepped inside. "Just make yourself at home. I'll be a minute." With another flash of smooth leg, she moved into the bedroom and closed the door.

As he waited for her to return, he moved tentatively around the living room. At some point over the last seven years, the room had been redecorated in bold shades of green, yellow and orange. The bright colors breathed life into the small room.

He moved over to an end table where several framed pictures rested. There was one of her mother standing in front of the puppet theater, her smile much like Nikki's, wide and guileless. There was a picture of Nikki and Bridget together, sitting in the interior of the pizza place, their arms affectionately wrapped around each other.

The third one was of a man Grey didn't recognize. Grey picked up the photo, studying the man's face. Grey supposed by women's standards he would be considered handsome. Blond hair emphasized a deep tan and the blueness of his eyes. Although his full beard was neatly trimmed, it hid much of the lower portion of his face.

"That's Johnny, my ex-husband," she said from behind him.

He heard the slight catch in her voice and when he turned around and looked at her, her eyes were filled with a fleeting pain. "Shall we go?" she asked tersely.

Carefully, he set the photo down, his heart clenching curiously in his chest. "Did you love him?" he asked without looking at her.

There was a moment of hesitation. "That's really none of your business," she returned unevenly. "In any case, it doesn't matter now. He's gone, a part of my past, and I make it a practice never to look back."

"Never?" he asked. Didn't she ever think about those days and nights with him? Didn't she remember how perfectly attuned their bodies had been, how right they had always felt in each other's arms?

"Never," she repeated with a finality that sounded like the closing of the chamber to a heart. "Shall we go?" She opened the door and looked at him expectantly.

As they walked toward the carnival lights and gaiety, Grey wondered what had happened to hurt her. Had her marriage been so bad? Had she loved her husband desperately and been devastated when they'd divorced?

He had so many questions he wanted to ask, so many things he needed answered. But he felt her tension.

He knew it would take next to nothing to send her running back to her house, and he didn't want to do that. For the time being, he'd play by her rules, let the questions from the past wait. But sooner or later, they would talk about what had happened.

He gazed at her from the corner of his eye, noting the tangle of hair that fell down her back, hair that always looked as if it could use a thorough brushing. Yet he knew that to his touch, it would be silky and thick and no amount of brushing and smoothing could tame the errant strands. His fingers itched to reach out and stroke it. Instead, he clenched his hands into fists at his sides.

He looked away, surprised by the intense bolt of desire that coursed through him. Funny, that even though he felt ill at ease with her and even though they were practically strangers now, his body remembered hers and rejoiced in the anticipation of a reunion.

"It certainly doesn't look like a dying amusement park tonight," he observed as they hit the walkway illuminated with colored lights.

"Saturday nights are our best nights. Last year, the economy was so bad and your father raised the rents. It was difficult for most of us to keep our heads above water. But we're hoping this will be a better summer . . . unless you have another rent increase in mind."

He sighed with a touch of irritation. "How many times do I have to remind you that I'm not my father?"

She looked at him speculatively. "I guess you'll have to show me with actions instead of telling me with words that your priorities are different from those of the other Blakemores."

"And what makes you think I'm any different than I was seven years ago?" he asked.

As she looked at him, her hazel eyes, so ever-changing in hue, were more green than usual. "I'm not sure I really knew you then, either."

Before he had a chance to ask her what she meant, they were in the middle of the midway and greetings inundated them from all sides.

"Hey, Nikki." Jim, the owner of the shooting gallery motioned her to his booth.

"I'll be back in just a minute," she said to Grey, then walked over to Jim and perched on the arm of his wheelchair. "What's up, Jimbo?" she asked, gazing affectionately at the paraplegic man who'd been a surrogate father to her for most of her life.

"What are you doing with him?" He nodded his head in Grey's direction.

"Trying to convince him not to close us down," Nikki replied.

"And what makes you think he's going to listen to you?" Jim asked dubiously.

"Nothing, except as president of the Boardwalk League, it's my job to try."

"Hmmph, he played you for a fool once. Are you going to let him do it again?"

"Of course not," she replied, a flush of emotion heating her face. "I learned my lesson very well."

Jim gazed at her warmly. "You aren't the first and you damn sure won't be the last. Since the boardwalk first opened wealthy young studs from town have been sowing their wild oats with the girls from the boardwalk. And as long as there are boardwalk girls and town boys, the cycle will continue."

Nikki bit down to still the instant protest that rose to her lips. It wasn't like that, she wanted to cry. What she and Grey had shared was more than just a town boy exploring his budding sexuality with his social inferior. Grey had been her friend, her companion, her soul mate. But even as her heart ached with these protests, her heart knew the truth. And the truth was she'd been a willing partner for sex.

When the chips were down, he'd tried to use his money to buy her off. After all, Blakemores didn't marry boardwalk brats.

She leaned over and kissed Jim on top of his bald head. "Don't you worry about me, Jimbo. Hurt me once, shame on you. Hurt me twice, shame on me. Believe me, the lesson was well learned. I'm not vulnerable to him anymore."

Jim stared at her for a long moment. "We're always vulnerable to the people we love."

Nikki stood up and smiled confidently. "Then I'm definitely safe because the only emotion I feel for Greyson Blakemore is hate. I'll work with him for the sake of the boardwalk, but I'll never stop hating him."

"Never is a long time, Cupcake."

"My hatred is strong. It will last a long time."

Again Jim cast her a dubious look. "I'd feel better if you felt nothing for him. Hatred is too close to love as far as I'm concerned."

"Not in this case," she confirmed. With another quick peck, this one on his cheek, Nikki left him and returned to where Grey stood watching a couple of teenagers trying to shoot baskets to win a huge stuffed dinosaur.

As she approached Grey, she found herself trying to study him objectively. He was still achingly attractive, damn him. And even though she wanted to hate everything about him, she couldn't deny that someplace deep inside her a flame of desire still burned brightly.

Their lovemaking had always been excruciatingly intense...an intensity that for Nikki had never been matched since. And she had to admit there was a part of her that wanted to experience it once more.

She'd lied to Jim. The emotion she felt for Grey wasn't just hatred. It was much more complex than that, mixed up with the kind of desire that was breath-stealing in potency.

Damn him, she thought again. A heated flush swept up her neck as he turned and smiled at her...a smile that might have melted her internal organs had she not steeled herself against its warmth.

"If I had back half of the money I spent at these booths, I could finance the boardwalk for the next fifty years," he said as she joined him.

"Nobody can resist the pull of games of chance. There's always the chance that for a mere dollar you could win the stuffed animal of your choice."

"Or the possibility that you'll spend a lot of dollars and come away empty-handed," Grey countered.

Nikki shrugged. "That's why they're called games of chance. It's all a gamble." Like love, she thought. Sometimes you roll a lucky seven and other times you shoot craps. "Come on, I'll take you over to the newest attraction."

He nodded and together they moved past booth after booth of skill and luck games. "You know, if you close down the boardwalk, you'll not only be displacing a lot of people, you'll also hurt Oceanview's economy," Nikki said. He looked at her curiously and she continued, "There isn't a teenage kid in Oceanview who hasn't at some point or another spent a summer working out here. The hotels and motels benefit from the tourists this amusement area attracts. So do the restaurants and fast-food chains."

"Nikki, does every sentence that comes out of your mouth have to be a defense for the boardwalk?"

"That's the issue at hand," she countered. "That's why I'm here with you now." She walked more briskly, realizing that being out here at night with Grey was dangerous.

The warm air, the salty smell of the sea, the flickering of the colorful lights overhead all evoked memories of the times when the night and the boardwalk had belonged to her and Grey.

They had enjoyed the rides until two in the morning when everything finally closed down, then they would run to their special place beneath the wooden walkway and make love until just before sunrise.

She mentally shook herself from the hold of memories. "The newest attraction on the board-walk," she said, pointing to where a large water slide loomed in the distance.

"I always thought there should be more water attractions," Grey observed as they approached the busy slide.

Together they stepped up on an observation platform that afforded them a perfect view of the kids careening down the twisting slide and splashing into a large pool at the bottom.

Nikki leaned against the railing, uncomfortably aware of Grey as he stood intimately close to her, so close his broad shoulder touched her. The hot night wind blew through her hair, whipping it across her face. She jumped as he leaned over and gently removed it, his fingertips lingering in its length for just a fraction too long.

"Thanks," she murmured, moving several steps away from him so she could no longer feel his body heat, smell the evocative scent of his cologne. "So when are you going to make up your mind about the boardwalk?" she asked, desperately clinging to the one and only topic she wanted to discuss with him. "We're all in limbo until you make a final decision."

"What will you do if I shut it down?" he asked.

"I'll survive," she answered. "It's not me I'm worried about. I'll get a job, move on, make a new life, but it won't be so easy on the others." Again the wind whipped her hair and she quickly tucked the errant strands behind her ears before he could take the opportunity to touch her again. She didn't want him touching her. It hurt and felt wonderful at the same time. "It's the people like Jim and Bridget that I worry about . . . the people society threw away because they didn't quite fit the norm."

She stared into his eyes, wanting to find some semblance of the man she'd once loved, wanting to seek out a small part of the boy who'd loved the boardwalk as much as she had. "That's always been the magic of the boardwalk . . . the fact that acceptance is a given despite anyone's physical limitations." She started to place her hand on his arm in an attempt to make him understand, but stopped before her fingers touched his flesh. Instead, she gazed back toward the slide.

"You know, you said something a little while ago that gave me an idea."

"What?" She looked at him curiously, wishing her mind would focus on the boardwalk issue and not on how good it felt to be standing next to him, breathing in his essence.

"Even though there are only a couple of miles that separate the boardwalk from Oceanview, the town and the boardwalk have always operated as completely separate entities. Yet you're right, the town depends on this area for much of its economy. Maybe it's time we get some sort of financial commitment from the people of Oceanview."

"Sounds like a wonderful idea, but how do we go about doing it?"

"I don't know, I'll have to think about it. Maybe a place to start is to give a dinner party and invite all the merchants from town. I think that would be a step in the right direction."

She nodded, encouraged by his words. She gazed out at the children on the slide, enjoying the sound of their excited laughter as they rode the slide to the pool of water beneath.

"Nikki...." His voice was a mere whisper that seemed to echo in the hollows of her mind.

She turned and looked at him, heat filling her up as she saw the flame that lit the centers of his eyes, a familiar flame that spoke of passion-filled caresses beneath the boardwalk. "You know what I think?" he said. "I don't think there ever was any real magic here." He stood so close to her, his breath gently fanned her face with the sweet scent of minty freshness and an underlying aroma of cotton candy. "I think the magic was always you and me together and not this place at all."

"Don't be ridiculous," she scoffed, but her voice sounded breathless and lacking conviction even to

her own ears. He stood so close to her it was difficult to think, difficult to do anything. "The magic
of the boardwalk is people working together
and...and sharing dreams...and taking care of
each other." She frowned, trying to remember all
that Bridget had told her, but the words were getting tangled up in her head, tangled in the sensations his proximity stirred. "I told you before...you
and me...that was youth and the excitement of two
innocents experimenting."

"But I'm not young or inexperienced now, so
why do I still want you like I did then?"

"Don't Grey, please," she begged, closing her
eyes against the onslaught of emotions that raged
inside her. "I told you I don't look back, and I
can't go back to that place in time." She drew a
deep breath and opened her eyes to look at him.

She wanted to rail at him, scream at him for
wanting to just pick up where they had left off so
long ago, as if he had done nothing to betray her
heart. But she knew that she had the future of many
people resting on her, and alienating Grey certainly wouldn't help their positions.

More than anything, she wished he'd step away
from her, distance himself so she could think ra-
tionally instead of focusing so many of her thoughts
on the shape of his mouth, the remembered heat
that had been contained there. "Grey, we're
strangers. Our lives have taken us in completely

different directions.'' She sighed again, suddenly weary.

''Nikki, I never forgot you. I can still remember the taste of your skin, the texture of it. I still remember each and every time we made love, each and every time you moaned my name.'' He placed his hands on her shoulders. ''Tell me you don't think about those nights under the boardwalk. Look at me and tell me you don't remember how right we felt together.'' His eyes burned into hers as his fingers tightened on her shoulders.

She drew upon the anger that was always just beneath the surface. She remembered her labor, so many hours of pain all alone. She thought of her joyous letter to him answered by an envelope of money. And finally she thought of their baby, now resting in the graveyard. She looked into his ember-colored eyes and lied. ''Never,'' she said firmly. Then, purposefully extricating herself from his hold, she turned and walked away.

Five

Nikki tossed and turned restlessly and threw the sheet off her perspiring body. Hot. In the hours since she had left Grey standing near the water slide, the night had gone from unseasonably warm to uncomfortably hot. She knew at least part of it was due to the outside temperature, but most of it was due to her own mental state.

Being with Grey had made her hot, had made her body ache with an emptiness she had refused to acknowledge for a very long time.

She'd had to leave when she did. She'd been desperately afraid that he might kiss her, and the thought of his lips touching hers both terrified and thrilled her.

With a sigh of frustration, she finally sat up, realizing sleep was an elusive oblivion. She was restless, filled with an energy she couldn't release and that refused to be ignored.

Expelling another deep sigh, she got out of bed and grabbed a short terry-cloth robe. Pulling it around her nakedness, she left the bedroom and went out the front door of the house, running desperately across the beach.

A swim was what she needed. A bracing, energetic swim that would exhaust the internal ache right out of her. If she was exhausted, she wouldn't remember. If she was exhausted, perhaps she wouldn't want him.

She shed the robe without breaking her stride, and dived into the moon-tipped waves like a porpoise seeking home. Her strokes were sure and strong, the water a numbing coldness that momentarily assuaged her body's heat.

How was it possible for hate and desire to coincide? she wondered as she rolled over on her back and floated atop the refreshing water. How was it possible for her to want Grey with a relentless longing that made her hate seem ineffectual as a defensive shield? Why were her mind and body working at cross-purposes, one trying to hold on to the bitterness while the other lusted for him?

She flipped over and increased her strokes, wanting the exhaustion to take away the craving her body suffered. But somehow she knew that she could swim the length and width of the ocean and her body would still yearn for his.

His kisses were her weakness, his caresses her addiction, and the memory of those kisses and caresses taunted her, tormented her.

Again she rolled over to float faceup, her mind sweeping her to the distant time, back into his arms. She not only remembered the first, awkward time they'd made love, she remembered every time afterward. Each time, their bodies had grown more attuned one to the other. They'd quickly learned the special places to touch, to kiss, the intimate little caresses that would evoke the most pleasure.

She groaned and choked as she swallowed a mouthful of the salty seawater. Reluctantly, she headed for shore, realizing that no amount of strenuous swimming could take away the heat that curled in her stomach.

As she walked out of the waves, she saw him. He stood in the place where he'd always waited for her when she'd swim in the moonlight.

He was partially hidden in the deep shadows of the boardwalk, but even from this distance she could see the glow of his eyes as they hypnotically beckoned to her.

She stood in the breaking waves, stunned as he stepped out of the shadows and into the moonlight. He was nude, and fully aroused.

Reality and space fell away as Nikki felt herself plummet backward in time. He was Grey, the man she'd loved more than life itself. The young man who'd always made her body sing and her soul smile. She couldn't fight against the waves of desire that washed over her, taking with them every other emotion except her powerful need for him.

She didn't move as he advanced toward her. She was afraid to try, afraid that her knees would buckle and she'd fall if she tried to take a single step. Her bones had the consistency of liquid jelly... hot molten lava had replaced her blood.

He stopped when he stood mere inches from her. Although he didn't touch her, she could feel the heat emanating from his body, smell the wild scent of him that wrapped around her.

With the tip of one finger, he reached out and lightly traced the swell of her bottom lip. Nikki moaned, caught in a place where past and present merged, where there was no room for thought, insane or rational. She only knew she wanted him... desperately wanted him one last time. She needed his magic one last time before she finally put him out of her life.

She captured his finger in the warmth and wetness of her mouth, heard the soft moan that escaped him. It was music to her soul, balm for her spirit.

In one smooth movement, he swept her up out of the waves and into his arms. He carried her to the shadowed darkness beneath the boardwalk, where a blanket covered the night-cooled sand. He gently laid her down, then stretched out beside her, not touching her physically, but searing her body with the heat of his gaze.

Again his fingers touched her mouth, tracing first the upper lip, then the lower with a feather-light graze. He leaned his head forward, his lips touching hers so softly, she felt as if it could be a dream. But it wasn't, it was wonderfully real and she wanted it, needed it to survive.

As she opened her mouth to him, he hungrily deepened the kiss, his tongue seeking and demanding. She answered the demand, returning the kiss with a fervor to match his.

As the kiss ended, he took his tongue and gently licked her lips, the eroticism evoking another moan of pleasure from her. She had forgotten how sensual Grey was. No, not forgotten, she amended. She'd suppressed the memory, always finding it too painful to examine.

However, memories of yesterdays were quickly usurped by the reality of this moment as his lips moved across the contours of her cheeks, down into the hollow of her neck. He touched her no place else, but Nikki's entire body tingled with the searing effect of his lips against her skin.

As his tongue found the sensitive flesh behind her ear, she gasped in pleasure and writhed, her hands clenching the blanket. Hot fire. His lips caused it to flame inside her, engulf her. A fireball of need grew to mammoth proportions, flaring brighter and brighter, obscuring all but the sensations his mouth produced.

The stars peeking through the cracks in the boardwalk overhead blurred together into a single starburst as his mouth moved down to her breast, his teeth lightly grazing the turgid nipple.

Nikki was vaguely aware that she should stop this . . . stop him. But she couldn't fight the raging winds of heat and light that pulsated inside her at his touch. She wanted this. She wanted him. Nobody had ever been able to make her feel this way. Nobody but Grey.

Besides, she rationalized with her last vestige of sanity, she wasn't seventeen years old anymore. She was older, wiser, able to handle this fleeting moment of passion and know it meant nothing to her heart.

As his tongue flicked at her other nipple, she let her protests die and simply gave herself to the mind-shattering power of his caresses.

He loved her with his mouth first, not touching her with any other portion of his body. His lips trailed down her flat abdomen, pausing to nip and taste every inch. She kept her hands clenched into the blanket until he reached the juncture of her thighs, then she tangled them into his hair and cried out as she rode the crest of the waves that suffused her.

Then it was her turn to love him. Without saying a word, she gently pushed him over on his back, her fever fed by the fire in his eyes and his obvious arousal.

It was the way they had always made love, teasing and taunting each other until neither could stand it another minute.

His flesh was hot, as if fevered, and as Nikki kissed down the broadness of his chest, she reveled in the feel of his sinewy muscles beneath the taut, bronzed skin. He tasted of the salty breeze and the hot night air, a taste of mystery and strength that had always belonged to him alone.

She kissed and licked down the flatness of his stomach, felt his muscles tense and coil as she continued her intimate caresses. From his stomach she moved directly to the top of his thighs, consciously ignoring the place where she knew he wanted her most. She kissed one thigh then the other, allowing her hair to sweep over his rigidness, reveling in the deep moans that echoed off the boards over their heads.

She leaned forward, allowing her breasts to rub against the curly hair of his chest. Oh, how she loved the feel of him, his skin against hers. She luxuriated in his scent and his taste.

The night breeze off the water merely intensified the erotic feel of skin on skin, increased the tactile pleasure of cool wind and warm flesh.

Grey was lost...lost to Nikki and the magic she'd always produced when she touched him. She was the essence of sexuality, her eyes gleaming with the abandon of a woman who loved her own sensuality.

He vaguely realized that was part of her enchantment, her complete acceptance of herself as a sexual being. Nikki was a free spirit, as impossible to tame as the wind, and to her, sex was as natural as breathing. It showed in her every caress, her every kiss. She was in touch with the primal side of herself in a way most people were not.

The vague thoughts skittered away, lost to something more powerful as her mouth finally, exquisitely surrounded him, engulfed him in heat and fire. He closed his eyes, shivers of pleasure racing through him. He tangled his hands in the length of her hair and moaned her name into the air.

He wanted it to last forever, but knew it couldn't...knew he couldn't. Already he felt the blood boiling inside him, surging with a ferocious power as his body spiraled toward release.

With a torturous groan, he lifted her up his body and rolled over, poised to bury himself in her velvet heat. He hesitated a moment, his gaze seeking hers, finding there the wildness that fed the savage passion in him.

Gently he eased himself inside, loving the way her eyes flared as he settled deep within her. He didn't move again for a moment or two, renewing his tenuous control so it wouldn't end too fast.

When he did finally move, it was with slow, languid strokes, withdrawing almost entirely, then filling her up completely.

It was like being sheathed in hot silk, and he trembled with the intensity of the sensations their union evoked. Even after all the years they'd been apart, their bodies remembered the rhythm of love, fell easily into the cadence that brought them both the most pleasure.

His lips found hers in a kiss of consuming hunger and her tongue battled with his in an erotic dance. Their groans of desire, their whimpers of delirium rode the wind and wafted out to mingle with the sounds of the breaking waves against the shore.

Grey felt himself losing the last modicum of control and increased the speed of his movements. She matched him, arching to meet his thrusts in a frenzied need of her own. He felt her body stiffen, knew the moment she reached her release. Her hands clutched convulsively at his back and she cried out his name. She shuddered for an endless moment and then he was there, joining her, feeling as if he died just a little as his body tensed and he cried out hoarsely with his own climax.

He collapsed to the blanket, shifting the bulk of his weight to one side. With a final shudder, he buried his face in the sweet flesh at the hollow of her neck, breathing in the scent of her.

She always smelled the way he'd thought the sun might smell—clean and fresh, the indefinable scent of hot sun and ocean breeze.

He felt the softness of her body as it tensed against him, knew the instant that regret entered her mind. He leaned up on one elbow, his hand automatically seeking the warm curve of her breast. At his touch she turned her head away.

"Nikki?"

She didn't move, didn't turn to look at him.

He hesitated, unsure exactly what he wanted to say. He was stunned by what they'd shared, amazed by the natural, all-consuming reunion their bodies had shared. Physically, they had moved together as if no time had passed, as if it had only been yesterday that they'd last made love.

There had been no awkward need to reacquaint, no clumsy fumbling of unwanted caresses. Their bodies hadn't registered the passage of time. It was as right now as it had been seven years ago, and again he wondered what had happened. How had they ever lost each other?

"Nikki, we need to talk," he finally said, wanting—needing—to understand what had happened to make them forget how special they were together, how important they'd been to each other.

She sat up, pushing his hand away from her. She crossed her arms over her breasts, her gaze searching the beach as if looking for something. Without answering him, she got up and walked a short distance. Bending over, she picked up the robe she'd discarded earlier and drew it around her.

This single action, more than anything, let Grey know the extent of the changes in her. The Nikki of his past would have never felt the need to cover her nakedness from him.

He panicked as he realized she had begun to walk away, back in the direction of her cottage. He jumped up, snatched his cutoffs and pulled them on.

He ran after her and grabbed one of her shoulders. "Nikki, I said we need to talk." He twirled her around to face him.

"Why?" The moonlight stroked her face, showing him the numbing emptiness that filled her eyes. "What's there to talk about, Grey?" A sharp burst of bitter laughter fell from her lips, only increasing the hollow bleakness of her gaze. "I was easy for you seven years ago and I guess after all this time, that one thing hasn't changed.''

He gasped in surprise. ''What the hell does that mean?'' he asked incredulously.

The emptiness in her eyes transformed, filling with a new emotion, a bitterness he didn't understand, couldn't comprehend. ''Everyone warned me years ago. Don't get involved with him, Nikki, they said. Town boys play with boardwalk girls, but they don't play fair. When it comes time for marriage and families, town boys always go with one of their own. Blakemores don't marry boardwalk brats.'' Her body vibrated as the words shot out of her, as if escaping despite an enormous inner pressure to keep them trapped. ''But I told everyone, Grey isn't like that. Grey is different.''

Her features contorted with a pain so intense, Grey's heart echoed the emotion even though he didn't understand what had caused it. ''You promised me forever,'' she cried angrily, her tortured voice filled with the pain of betrayal.

He stared at her, confused by her words, by her emotion. ''But you're the one who married while I was at college,'' he protested, a rising anger in him as he remembered when he'd heard of her marriage. ''It was you who couldn't wait for me, not the other way around,'' he finished accusingly.

She drew a deep breath, as if to steady herself. ''What else was I supposed to do? I was desperate.

I was alone and didn't know what to do.'' She closed her eyes for a moment and when she looked at him again, he felt the burning anger she directed at him. "I refused to even consider an abortion and I didn't want the baby to be illegitimate. Johnny offered to marry me and give the baby his name. What else was I supposed to do? I was so scared.''

"Wait...." Grey held up his hands to still her, his head reeling. "What are you talking about? What baby?''

"Our baby. The one you wanted me to abort.'' The words spat out of her as tears spilled onto her cheeks. "The one you sent me money to take care of.''

Grey felt as if the world was shifting beneath his feet. He placed a hand on his forehead and stumbled, as if the sand had momentarily displaced and thrown him off balance. Her words whirled around and around in his head, filling him with confusion. "Nikki, what in God's name are you talking about? I swear I don't understand. What baby? What money?'' He stared at her, not comprehending any of it.

Some of the anger seemed to seep out of her and she eyed him dubiously, uncertainly. "I wrote to you, Grey. The day I found out, I wrote and told you that I was pregnant, and you sent me back an envelope filled with money.''

"I never got your letter and I never sent you anything," he answered, a dull roar resounding in his ears as he tried to sort out events that had happened so many years ago. "I . . . I don't understand any of this. When did you send me a letter? Do you remember when you sent it?"

A bitter smile curved her lips. "Oh, yes, I remember the date quite well. You would have received the letter in the first week of October."

Grey frowned, trying to sift through the memories and echoes of time, attempting to find reason in the madness he felt surrounding him. "The first week in October? That was always my parents' weekend at the college. My father. . . ."

He stared at her bleakly, hollowly, suddenly able to fathom what had happened, who had ultimately received her letter and who had sent her the money. "My God, my father . . . he must have gotten the letter. He must have sent the money."

Pain and bitterness ripped through him. He roared a cry of impotent anger, raising his face to the sky to curse the fates.

He swallowed a sob and turned to look at Nikki. "I didn't know," he whispered harshly. "Don't you see? I didn't know." He crossed to her, started to reach for her, but dropped his hands to his sides as she stepped back from him.

"It doesn't matter," she said dully, and he saw the numbing emptiness return to her eyes. "It's too late. It's long over and done. It simply doesn't matter anymore.''

"What do you mean it doesn't matter? Of course it matters. The baby...you didn't...surely you couldn't....'' He let the questions trail off, afraid of her answer, his heart feeling as if it might explode in his chest.

"Have an abortion?'' She shook her head and wrapped her arms around herself. "No, Grey, I didn't have an abortion. I couldn't. I wanted the baby more than I ever wanted anything in my life.''

Grey expelled a sigh of relief and felt a surge of joy fill him up. A child. He and Nikki had a child. It was like a gift from heaven, a treasured remnant of the past and their innocent love.

He rubbed his forehead, emotion whirling, questions demanding answers. "Do...do I have a son or a daughter?'' So many questions. Where was the baby? No, not a baby, a child...a six-year-old child. "I guess he's not a baby anymore. He must be in school.'' Excitement, happiness rippled through Grey, causing his words to tumble over one another. "He's old enough to ride on my shoulders...old enough to call me Daddy—''

"We had a daughter, Grey,'' Nikki interrupted tersely. "A beautiful little girl.'' He heard the words as they caught in her throat, and an inexplicable dread coursed through him, swallowing his initial joy.

He swallowed thickly, suddenly afraid. "What happened? Where...where is she? Where is she now?" Had Nikki given their daughter up for adoption? Oh, God, was the child forever lost to them? Had he discovered the truth too late? His heart beat frantically in his chest as he waited for her to answer.

She hesitated, sorrow pulling her features downward. Moonlight captured the single tear that fell to her cheek. She turned away from him, her eyes no longer meeting his. "I named her Lolly...Lolly Richards." She spoke softly, and he moved a step closer to her in order to hear. "She was stillborn, Grey. You'll find her in the Land's End graveyard." Her voice was flat, empty, devoid of all emotion. "She's dead, Grey. Our daughter is dead."

This time, as Nikki slowly turned and walked away, Grey didn't try to stop her. He couldn't. He was caught in a maelstrom of emotions so intense, he was frozen in time, in space, able only to stand and watch her as she disappeared into the darkness of the night.

Six

_____

Nikki watched the sun rise from her front porch, wishing she could swallow the yellow ball of fire to warm her insides. She'd never been so cold in all her life, and never had she felt such emptiness...a vast abyss deep within that yawned like a black hole of nothingness.

Before last night, she'd at least had her anger to buoy her, her bitterness to keep the grief at bay. Now that Grey had taken that, she was frightened, scared of what emotions she might face once the numbing emptiness went away.

He hadn't known about the baby. He'd never known. He hadn't betrayed her. He'd had nothing to do with it. The words reverberated inside her head, echoed in her heart. Although they should have filled her up with a kind of joy, they didn't. They merely made her sorrow deeper, her vague dreams of what might have been more intense.

Last night's lovemaking had added to her confusion and sense of loss. This morning, her body was fulfilled, sated by the depth of his lovemaking. But her heart was still as empty, as cold as ever. And she simply didn't know what to do to make her heart warm again.

Overwhelmed by her turmoil, she went into the house and made coffee. As she watched the dark liquid drip through the machine and into the glass carafe, she wondered what would happen next.

Somehow, she had the feeling that nothing had changed between her and Grey. Although her bitterness and anger against him had eased, the result of their shared past was still too painful to overcome. Even though he hadn't known about Lolly, it didn't change the reality of her death and Nikki's deep, abiding grief.

The fact that Thomas Blakemore had been able to manipulate them so easily only pointed to the fact that their love hadn't been strong enough to trust in. They hadn't questioned the circumstances. When she had received the money, she'd never doubted that it came from Grey. And when he had received his letters back from her unopened, he hadn't questioned that for some reason she'd fallen out of love with him. Their love hadn't been enough for them to seek out each other, discuss what was happening. They'd allowed circumstances and a wicked old man to destroy them.

And now, too much time had passed and their baby's death would always remain between them, a tragedy Nikki would never be able to put behind her.

She sighed heavily and poured herself a cup of coffee, knowing that even though they had managed to straighten out much of the tangled events of the past, it had done nothing to ease the strain of the present.

Grey was waiting for his mother when she came downstairs for breakfast. "Good morning," she said, smiling pleasantly as she went to the sideboard and poured herself a cup of coffee from the silver server.

"We need to talk," he said without preamble.

"Is something wrong, dear?" She joined him at the table, looking at him curiously.

"I had a long talk with Nikki Young last night." As he watched, the smile on his mother's face faded, crumbling into one of dread. "Did you think I wouldn't find out?" he demanded, untouched by the sudden vulnerability that pinched his mother's features. "Did you honestly believe I could come back here and not find out that she'd had my child?"

"I told your father not to get involved. When he took her letter from your mail at school, I begged him not to interfere." Her voice trembled and her gaze didn't quite meet his. "I told him to let you work it out yourself. But he was certain Nikki had bewitched you. He said that you would drop out of school, destroy your life by marrying her."

"I loved her." Grey stared at his mother incredulously. "I loved her more than anyone else, and she needed me and I wasn't there for her. Whatever I might or might not have done, it should have been my decision." He clenched his hands into fists on the tabletop, looking down at the lacy pattern of the cloth. "That baby was your grandchild. For God's sake, didn't that mean anything to you?" He looked back up at her.

His mother drew a deep, tremulous breath, and when she looked at him, her eyes were filled with glistening tears. "There isn't a day that passes that I don't think of that baby and Nikki and pray for forgiveness. That was the one time in my life I should have stood up to your father, but old habits die hard. I simply didn't know how to stand up to him.''

As Grey looked at her, his anger with her whooshed out of him. She was as much a victim as everyone else. Grey knew the iron hand Thomas Blakemore had used to rule his household, knew the power the old man had exerted over everyone, including Grey's mother. She didn't deserve his anger... only a kind of pity. He sighed and stood up.

"Where are you going? What are you going to do?'' she asked worriedly, her bottom lip quivering uncontrollably as she gazed up at him.

Grey ran a hand through his hair. "I'm going to the graveyard to visit my daughter and then...then I don't know what I'll do.'' With that, he turned and left.

This time, as he walked toward Land's End, he didn't run. Instead, his footsteps were slow and plodding, like those of an old man. He felt as if he'd aged a million years since the night before.

His eyes were gritty with lack of sleep and his heart was so heavy it lay in the pit of his stomach. He'd never felt so old, so utterly disillusioned.

All the wasted years. All the moments that had been stolen from him. When Nikki had returned his letters, he should have come home, discovered what was happening.

If only he'd done that. If only he'd come back and confronted Nikki. If only...if only...

He frowned, realizing why he hadn't. Nikki had been like a treasure in his life. She'd been the most vivid, real thing he'd ever experienced, and not a day of his youth had passed when he hadn't marveled that she wanted him, loved him.

At a young age, Grey had recognized the selfishness and greed that was his legacy from his father, and Nikki with her giving spirit and absolute selflessness had been a gift...a gift he somehow feared he didn't deserve.

He shoved these thoughts aside as he reached the gates of the Land's End Cemetery. The moment he walked through the gates, an oppressive lump balled up in his chest, causing his breaths to grow shallow, more difficult.

He walked past the older graves, his footsteps slowing to a snail's pace. The cemetery was small and it didn't take him long to find his daughter's grave.

Last night, when Nikki had told him of the baby and the death, it had all seemed like a horrible nightmare. Now, standing over the tiny headstone, the reality slammed into him with a force that momentarily knocked the breath out of him.

Lolly Richards. Lolly. His heart convulsed and he clenched his hands at his sides, taking shallow breaths as he tried to fight against the pain.

Lolly. For Lollipop. He and Nikki had spent long hours talking about the children they would one day have... children they'd laughingly said they'd name Lollipop and Moonbeams.

Nikki had followed through on their youthful imaginings, but he hadn't been here with her... for her. He tried to imagine the anguish she must have suffered, the long, painful hours of labor for nothing but a grave.

He couldn't imagine, but his heart ached with the knowledge that he should have been here sharing the grief with her. She'd grieved alone. He should have been with her, at least he would have been able to hold her, love her, share the sorrow with her. Yes, she'd grieved alone and now he was left to grieve the same way... alone.

He bent down and pulled a handful of weeds, focusing on the physical activity rather than the emotions that roiled inside him. He wasn't ready to face the brunt of his emotions. They were too powerful, too strong. He wasn't ready to face his grief. It was still too new, too raw.

The cemetery was in bad shape, overgrown and filled with weeds and brush. He made a mental note to call somebody about mowing it.

He heard footsteps before he saw anyone. He stood up just as Nikki broke through the clearing near the entrance gates. As their gazes met and held for a moment, Grey's heart exploded with a renewed surge of pain. She gasped, obviously surprised by his presence, then turned and disappeared the way she had come.

Grey hesitated only a moment before following her, needing her more than he'd ever needed anyone in his life.

It took her only moments to reach her cottage, but she knew he was right behind her. She wasn't surprised when he knocked and called her name through the door. For a moment, she stood frozen in the center of the living room, unsure what to do.

"Nikki, please let me in," he called softly, and suddenly she knew it was right that he'd come. It was right that they finally share their grief, talk about the little girl that might have been, their life together that should have been.

She opened the door, not saying a word, taking her cue from him. "Nikki." He breathed her name softly and in three strides he was through the door and had her gathered in his arms.

She closed her eyes, felt tears welling up in the corners. She breathed in the clean scent of him, reveling in the warmth and comfort she felt in his embrace. She buried her face in the broadness of his chest as his hands pressed her more tightly against the length of him. Oh, yes, this was what she had needed for so very long . . . to grieve and talk to the man who had been the father of her little girl.

She suddenly realized how desperately she needed to talk about Lolly with him. Immediately after the birth, she'd wanted to talk about the baby to anyone who'd listen. "Don't dwell on it," they'd replied. "Put it behind you." In her friends' well-meaning attempts to alleviate her pain, they'd only managed to make her bury it inside her where it festered like an infected sore. But she needed to dwell on it with Grey.

"Oh, Nikki." He sighed. The deepness of the sigh stirred her hair and echoed inside her. She felt the heaviness of his heart, and in some way it helped alleviate some of the heaviness of her own.

She looked up at him, into the somber dark hues of his eyes. "You want to talk?" she asked unevenly.

He shook his head. "No, I need ... I want...." With a slight moan, his lips claimed hers in savage intensity, causing her breath to catch in her throat.

She tasted his need, rampant and wild and it called on a mirrored need in her. She knew what he was doing, tamping down his grief, refusing to acknowledge it in favor of losing himself in the act of renewing life.

As he swept her up in his arms, she clasped her hands together around his neck, hoping that finally, together, they could ride this emotional storm and begin the first stages of healing.

He carried her into her bedroom, where her bed was unmade and a light morning breeze ruffled the gauzy curtains at the window.

He placed her on the bed, for a moment looming over her, his eyes tumultuous with suppressed emotion. She saw myriad feelings there—rage and sorrow, passion and remorse—like a simmering cauldron, his eyes reflected what had been inside Nikki for seven long years.

She placed a hand on the side of his face, realizing that she still cared about him. Despite the years, despite the pain, something of what she'd once felt for him still remained.

He leaned over her, his fingers fumbling to unbutton her blouse. She didn't help him, instinctively knowing he didn't want her to. When he'd removed her garment, he slid her slacks off her hips and down the length of her legs. He tossed them onto the floor, his gaze darkening as it lingered on her. His gaze alone had the power to make her nipples surge against the lacy confines of her bra.

He stepped away from the side of the bed and pulled his shirt over his head. Still looking at her, he unzipped his pants, the sound of the zipper breaking the utter silence in the room.

Again Nikki felt her breath catch as he stepped out of his slacks and briefs. The symmetry of his masculine body overwhelmed her.

Last night in the moonlight, she'd had little visual pleasure in making love to him. But now, the sunshine streamed through the windows, painting his gorgeous body with lush gold tones of light and warmth.

The sight of him, so bold, so beautiful, aroused her tremendously, and with a small cry she held out her arms to him, wanting him beside her, inside her. Their talk could wait until later. Right now, she needed the healing magic of his body next to hers.

He hesitated a moment, a frown puckering his forehead. "Nikki, I don't have anything...any protection."

Last night, there had been no thought of protection, the need to prevent a pregnancy. Now, with thoughts of Lolly in his head, she knew he didn't want a repeat of history.

She shook her head. "It doesn't matter. There were complications...the doctor told me I can't get pregnant again."

Pain, swift and ripe twisted his features. Nikki reached out and took his hand. She kissed his fingertips. "It's all right," she said softly.

He joined her on the bed and it took him only a moment to remove her underclothes. Almost like magic the two wisps of silk disappeared, leaving her vulnerable and aching for his touch.

His lips sought hers, as full of voltage as a live wire. The kiss created tingles racing through her, traveling the length of her body and back again. Desire surged, blotting out all else as his tongue battled with hers. She moaned in abandon as she felt him, hot and eager against her thigh.

She reached down and touched him, closing her hand around him. His breath hissed out and he groaned her name, his eyes flaming a fire out of control.

Unlike last night, she knew this time there would be little foreplay. His need was too great, too intense. But it didn't matter. She was ready for him and as he moved on top of her, she opened beneath him, welcoming his hardness into her warmth.

Grey moved like a man possessed, needing to lose himself in her. With little finesse he took her, buried himself in her, aching with the emotional demand to be close to Nikki, steal away some of her warmth and aliveness to battle the encroaching darkness his grief cast inside him.

He wanted to lose himself in sensations, take them both to a place where sorrow and grief had no substance, no power to hurt them anymore. He wanted to chase away the sorrow of death, push away the anguish and guilt that tore at his insides with relentless energy.

He drove into her, luxuriating in the exquisite feel of velvet and silk, fire and magic. She writhed beneath him, her eyes closed as tiny whimpers of pleasure escaped her lips. He placed his lips over hers, wanting to capture those whimpers in his mouth.

She locked her legs behind him, allowing him deeper, more fully into her. He moaned his pleasure, increasing his strokes. His urgency seemed to feed the same in her. She rocked with him, arching to meet him, encouraging him to go faster, deeper, harder.

Then he was lost in the magic that was life...and love...and Nikki.

Nikki opened her eyes, immediately realizing she'd fallen asleep. Next to her, Grey's even breathing told her he was asleep, too. She turned her head slightly so she could look at him in slumber.

The promise of handsomeness in youth had been realized. He'd been good-looking as a boy, a heartthrob as a teenager, but he was devastating in maturity. His lashes, so sinfully long and dark, shadowed the skin just beneath his eyes. His chin and cheeks were shadowed, as well, with the coarse stubble of a shaveless morning.

They must have been asleep for some time. The cast of the sun through the window, along with the heat, let her know it was afternoon. She knew she should get up, head for the theater. It was probably close to time for the first performance. But the warmth of Grey's arms around her, the intimacy of lying naked against him was too great for her to fight. She wanted to remain exactly where she was forever.

She tensed and shoved that particular word out of her mind. She didn't think in terms of forever anymore. Once upon a time, she had believed...and those dreams of happily-ever-after had been shattered and buried.

She started to get up, pausing as his arms tightened around her, letting her know he was awake. She turned over and found herself gazing into his eyes...eyes darkened with the lingering effect of pent-up feelings.

"I'm not going to sell the boardwalk," he said softly, reaching to stroke a strand of her hair away from her face. "I'll keep it going one way or another."

Nikki caught his hand in hers. "Grey, don't do it for me."

He brought her hand to his lips and gently kissed it, the darkness of his eyes lifting somewhat. "I'm not. I'm doing it for myself." He rolled over on his back and stared at the ceiling.

Nikki propped herself up on an elbow. "And don't do it for spite, Grey. Your father is dead. Keeping the boardwalk open to somehow vindicate the sins of your father won't do anything to change the past."

"I know that," he agreed. "But I also know that there *is* a magic here, a magic that I thought I'd outgrown. And I suddenly realize I need this place as much as it needs me." He turned his head to gaze at her, his eyes soft as the wings of a dove. "Can we pick up the pieces, Nikki? Can we go back and re-capture what was stolen from us?"

Nikki rolled over on her back, too, her gaze go-ing to the ceiling as if she might find the answer to his question there. "I don't know, Grey. So much time has passed. I've changed. I'm sure you have, too. We're not the same people we were seven years ago."

Grey leaned up over her, his hand gently closing around one of her breasts. "Nikki, despite the years, you can't ignore that something very strong still exists between us. I can't let it go. I don't want to let it go."

A sigh escaped her, a sigh of longing mingled with regret. "Oh, Grey, the sex between us was al-ways terrific. We've always been particularly at-tuned to each other in that respect."

"It's more than that," he protested. "It always was more than that. We had hopes and dreams."

"The hopes and dreams of youth," she re-minded him. "They were strong and beautiful in the summer, but couldn't sustain their strength in the autumn." Despite the fact that she'd made love with him twice in the last two days, she was afraid of the intimacy he now asked from her.

She'd lost her hope for happiness long ago, and the hope he held out to her frightened her. "Grey, we can't go back," she finally replied, her voice heavy. She'd learned to live without him and feared if she gave him her heart once again and it didn't work out, she wouldn't have the strength to survive.

"But we can go forward." He captured her chin in his hand, forcing her to look at him. "We can go forward from this moment in time, put the past to rest and explore what our future holds. Nikki, we owe it to each other to at least try. We owe ourselves another chance."

She stared into his eyes, wanting to reach out and seize the sweet promise that shone there. But she couldn't forget how easily they had crumbled before. Their love had been pure and wonderful, innocent and sweet. They'd believed in it's strength, but it had been an illusion, like the magic of the boardwalk.

But she couldn't deny that more than anything, she wanted him in her life, sharing those ancient dreams and hopes she'd buried so deep inside her. And, too, she had the feeling that if she didn't give them one final chance, she would forever be trapped in bitterness and would never grow beyond that.

She laughed, suddenly struck with how ludicrous the entire conversation was in their present condition. "It seems pretty silly to be talking about renewing our relationship while lying naked in each other's arms."

He smiled and traced the line of her lips with his fingertip. "Oh, Nikki, I've missed your laughter in my life."

She sobered. "It's been a long time since I've felt like laughing." She sat up and sighed. "Grey, if we're going to keep seeing each other, if we're going to try to build something between us, then we need to go slow. We've reacquainted ourselves sexually, but we've done very little to get to know what sort of people we've become." She looked at him searchingly. "We need to stay out of bed long enough to find out if we even like each other."

"Whew, I don't know about that." He grinned wickedly, mischievously, then his tone became serious. "There's always been something about you that makes me ache, Nikki." He stroked the smooth skin of her back, his fingers sparking trails of heat where they touched. "But if that's the way you want it, I'll try to control myself and the effect you have on me."

She arched against the heat of his touch, a renewed burst of desire sweeping through her as his fingers continued their sensuous exploration of her skin. "Then it's a deal," she said breathlessly as his lips followed the path of his fingers. "We'll see each other, follow through on what we began before, but we won't make love again until we see where we're going, how we feel about each other."

"It's a deal," he mumbled, his mouth moving, licking and kissing the length of her back. "But we'll start this new deal later," he said as he gently eased her back on the bed and his hands reached to caress her breasts. "Much later," he added, his gaze hot with need . . . with desire.

"Later," Nikki echoed, giving herself to the rising heat he stirred in her, surprised that so quickly after her being sated, he could stir a renewed ache inside her.

Seven

It wasn't until late afternoon that Grey left her house. As Nikki watched him walk away, she realized not once had he mentioned Lolly. Not once had the little girl's name fallen from his lips. It was as if the baby's death had no effect on him at all.

It doesn't matter, she told herself. It's all over and done with. It was time to move on. She needed to put the past behind her, where it belonged.

At least she could tell everyone that the boardwalk wouldn't close down. If nothing else good came out of this, at least that had been accomplished.

As far as she and Grey were concerned, she knew now that he owned a piece of her too great to ignore. She didn't have the strength to keep him out of her life. She didn't know what would happen as they tried to pick up the pieces and go on. She wasn't sure it was even possible for them to recapture what they'd once had. She only knew he was right, they owed it to themselves to try.

She would give him what she could—her body, her laughter, the pieces of herself she could afford to lose. But she couldn't give him her heart. That had been buried along with Lolly.

With a heavy sigh, she turned and went into the bedroom to get ready for her first performance at the puppet theater.

"I'm sure you've all heard by now that I've decided not to sell the boardwalk." Grey stood at the front of Bridget's back room, speaking to a large group of people gathered there at his request. "For the past two weeks, Nikki and I have been looking over the area, assessing what kind of work needs to be done to attract more of the tourist trade."

"How much is it gonna cost us?" Pete yelled, the worried question echoed by dozens more.

As Grey attempted to answer each question, Nikki watched him, marveling at how easily he led the crowd to see his dreams, believe in his hopes. He was charismatic...she'd always loved that about him. He was a natural-born leader and had probably been very successful in running the Blakemores's New York business interests.

In the past two weeks, Nikki had had the full effect of his charm. They'd spent the days cataloging the repairs that needed to be accomplished, listing new equipment that would spruce up the amusement park. Most nights he'd show up at the puppet theater at the end of the last performance, then they'd spend the nights enjoying the rides and booths until the park closed.

Those nights had been magical, like a journey back into the past. Those nights ended with a ride on the Ferris wheel, his arm around her as they reached the peak of the ride, Land's End spread out before them in glorious sparkling lights. At those moments, suspended far above the earth, Nikki would feel herself leaning into him, falling under his spell once again.

Their conversation became a sharing of the last seven years, as if they needed to fill each other in on every moment they had been separated.

True to their agreement, he hadn't tried to take her to bed; in fact, he hadn't kissed her since the last time they'd made love. He'd been most circumspect in that regard, and she hated it.

Even now, watching him as he stood so tall and handsome, she wanted him with a passion that couldn't be denied...like an itch she couldn't reach to scratch. She wondered if there would ever come a time when she didn't want him.

There were so many things about him she'd forgotten. His marvelous, full-bodied laugh, the way his forehead crinkled in the center when he frowned, the dusting of freckles the sun always painted on his shoulders.

She was remembering all the things she'd loved about him, and that scared her. She didn't want to love Grey, not with the same intensity, not with the same passion she'd once felt.

It was like being out of control, the same as the grief she'd never completely allowed herself to feel. That, too, felt like a loss of control.

She stirred from her thoughts as Bridget sidled up next to her. "How are you doing, honey?" she whispered as she placed an arm firmly around Nikki's waist. "I've hardly seen you in the last couple of weeks."

Nikki smiled. "Grey has kept me busy making lists. We're going to save it, Bridget. Grey is determined to save Land's End."

"I knew you would make him see it our way."

"He would have come to the same conclusion without me, he loves this place as much as we all do," Nikki exclaimed. She looked to where Grey was explaining to the crowd his plan to involve the town of Oceanview in the financial backing of the boardwalk.

"It appears the two of you have finally managed to resolve the past," Bridget observed.

Nikki looked at Grey. Had they managed to resolve the past? "Most of it," she finally answered hesitantly. But Nikki knew there were important pieces that hadn't been resolved, hadn't even been mentioned.

Bridget motioned for Nikki to follow her into the relative privacy of the kitchen. Once there, she looked at Nikki curiously. "So what's going on between the two of you...aside from your crusade to save the boardwalk?"

Nikki shrugged. "We're seeing each other, taking things very slow."

"I knew it," Bridget exclaimed, her eyes sparkling brilliantly. "I knew the two of you belonged together forever."

"Not forever," Nikki quickly protested. "One day at a time. That's as far in the future as I'm willing to look...especially with Grey."

"But you love him, and he loves you," Bridget said.

"No, we *loved* each other," Nikki corrected her firmly. "Past tense. We loved what we once had, dreams that were shattered by Grey's father and his manipulations."

"But you told me Grey had no part of that. He was as much a victim as you."

"That's true." Nikki agreed, then sighed, finding it difficult to put words to the vague stirring of unease still residing in her heart. Although things were going well between her and Grey, things were far from perfect. "Even though I know Grey was innocent in everything that happened before, I can't allow myself to believe in a forever with him."

"You mean because town boys don't marry boardwalk brats?" Bridget snorted her irritation. "That's a lot of nonsense. You're as good—better—than most of the townspeople I've ever met."

"I know that," Nikki agreed. "Grey never made me feel less than his social equal." She sighed. "The past two weeks with Grey have been wonderful. We've rediscovered a lot of the magic that once existed between us, but somehow it's been tainted....." She broke off in frustration. "I can't explain it. I can't even identify it. I just know that there's a part of me that can't let go of the past...can't get beyond the pain and bitterness I felt. It's encased my heart in ice, and until that's gone, I can't think in terms of forever or of loving Grey."

"Are you afraid of being hurt again?" Bridget asked tentatively.

Nikki shook her head. "No. I'm no longer seventeen years old and pregnant. No matter what happens between Grey and me, I won't be hurt. This time, I have no expectations. I'm a big girl. I can take what I want from him, enjoy his companionship, and whatever the end result, I will survive.''

"Sounds coldhearted to me," Bridget observed, worry in her eyes.

Nikki thumped her chest. "I told you, it's encased in ice." She hugged Bridget. "Don't worry, I'm much wiser this time around." They both turned as the door to the kitchen swung open and Grey walked in.

"I wondered where the two of you had disappeared to."

"Is the meeting over?" Nikki asked, releasing her hold on Bridget.

"For the time being. There were a lot of questions I couldn't answer until after the dinner party this evening."

"What dinner party?" Bridget asked.

"Grey and his mother are giving a dinner party this evening to broach the subject of financial support for the boardwalk to the merchants of Oceanview," Nikki explained.

"They've never done much to support us before," Bridget said dubiously. "In fact, they've always pretty much pretended like we didn't exist."

"They've never had to deal with me before," Grey returned with a grin. "And I intend to change all that. How about some lunch?" he asked Nikki.

"I'll have the ovens fired up in just a few minutes," Bridget exclaimed, donning an apron over her floral print dress.

"Actually, I was thinking of someplace away from the boardwalk."

He looked at Nikki, who shrugged. "Sounds good to me, as long as I'm back at the theater in time for the first performance."

"Well then, get going," Bridget demanded, shooing them out of the kitchen and into the mid-morning sunshine.

"So where to?" Nikki asked as they got into Grey's sports car.

"I don't know…I thought we'd drive a little ways up the coast and stop at the first restaurant that looks interesting." Grey grinned at her. "For the past two weeks, my food intake has been confined to boardwalk fare, and although I love it, I'm hungry for something more substantial than hot dogs and pretzels."

"Hmm, like a boiled lobster or steamed crab," Nikki said. Her stomach rumbled hungrily as she settled back in the luxury of the leather seat.

"Perhaps I should put the top up?" he asked before they hit the highway that would carry them along the coastline.

"Not on my account," she replied. She shook her head, her hair flying in abandon. "I love the wind."

Grey focused his attention on his driving, knowing well Nikki's love for the wind. She was like a part of the wind, a piece of nature bottled up in warm flesh and surging blood.

He gazed at her surreptitiously, as always captivated by her wild essence... an untamed soul that called to a like fragment inside him.

For seven years, he hadn't realized that he'd been half-dead. It had only been since his reunion with Nikki that full-bodied life once again surged in his veins.

She made him believe that life was full of endless possibilities, that dreams could become realities. She made him believe in rainbows and promises, in unicorns and moonbeams.

And yet, as wonderful as he felt when he was with her, he was aware of the fact that something was missing. Their innocence had been destroyed and there was now a piece of Nikki he couldn't reach, a piece of herself she guarded. He knew until he breached that area, which she so jealously protected, the real magic they'd always found would remain forever lost.

Time, he told himself. It was going to take time. She'd had seven years to hate him, seven years to believe he'd betrayed her in the worst possible way. He couldn't hope to overcome those seven years of negativity in a couple of weeks. He had to be patient.

He glanced at her again, noting the way the wind molded her T-shirt to the fullness of her breasts. His palms tingled with the remembered sensation of their satiny feel and he could smell the fresh, clean scent that emanated from her.

He tightened his grip on the steering wheel. Patience . . . it had never been one of his strong suits.

"It's beautiful out here, isn't it?" Nikki observed, pointing to the landscape of beach and ocean. The sunlight sparkled off the water, reflecting the cloudless blue sky overhead.

"I hadn't realized how much I missed it all when I was in New York. I didn't understand how much a part of me it was until I came back."

Nikki smiled at him, the wide, free smile that always made a coil of heat unfurl in his chest. "Ah, the boardwalk captures you when you're young, then never completely lets you go."

"Hopefully, with the help of Oceanview, we won't have to let it go," Grey observed.

"I'm surprised that your mother agreed to be a part of this dinner-party scheme of yours."

"Don't paint my mother with the same brush as my father." Grey sighed. "The most difficult thing I've had to face over the past couple of weeks is the fact that my father had the capacity to do something so heinous. I knew he was a control freak, a wealthy miser who used his money for power, but I always believed that somewhere inside was a good heart. I overlooked his faults, thinking his bottom line was love. But a man who could do to us what he did, had no concept of love.''

''Oh, Grey.'' She reached out and placed a hand on his arm, the warmth of it igniting a rapid brushfire in the pit of his stomach. ''Don't be too hard on him. I'm sure he did what he did with love for you in mind. I was a boardwalk brat, raised like a wild child without much structure or many rules. I'm sure the thought of your being involved with me scared the hell out of your father.'' She laughed suddenly. ''It's funny, your father didn't think I was good enough for you, and the people of the boardwalk thought you weren't good enough for me.''

''And in truth, we were perfect for each other.''

''At least at that time in our lives,'' she qualified, as if reminding him that the special time had passed and she wasn't sure how they fit together now.

''You know, Nikki, it never mattered to me where you came from. What mattered to me was who you were, how you made me feel when we were together.''

She nodded, withdrawing her hand from his arm, distancing herself across the seat. She hesitated a moment, then smiled at him. ''And it never mattered to me, either, because I knew the boardwalk people were right. I probably *was* far too good for you."

He laughed, knowing she was consciously changing the intimate course the conversation had taken. "Anyway, as of this morning, my mother was bustling around, talking with the caterers, preparing floral arrangements. She thrives on social activity."

"I should help do something. After all, this whole bash is for the boardwalk's benefit."

Grey shrugged. "She wanted to do it all. Perhaps it's her penance . . . her way of atoning for the past." He broke off and focused on his driving, wondering when they would be able to talk about the past without the edge of tension that always appeared as if from nowhere, standing between them like an invisible barrier.

He felt her gaze on him, felt a curious expectancy, but he didn't know what she wanted from him. "How about lunch there?" He pointed ahead where a weathered inn stood near the edge of the ocean, a sign proclaiming the establishment to be the Rusty Clipper.

"Looks good to me," she agreed.

Inside, the restaurant was exactly what Grey had wanted . . . darkly cool, quietly intimate, the redolence of good cooking in the air. They were led to a table in the corner, a private alcove with hanging plants and a candle burning in the center of the table.

"This is nice," Nikki said softly, opening the menu and scanning the pages.

"It is, isn't it," he agreed, noting how the candlelight danced in the length of her hair, made her eyes sparkle brightly.

He'd wanted to get her away from the boardwalk. When they were there, their conversation seemed to revolve around the work that had to be done. He wanted to get her away from there and talk about where they had been the past seven years, where they were going in the future. He wanted to talk to her about everything and nothing, about politics and religion, about the wind and the sea.

He needed to find out if the magic between them was a part of the boardwalk or if it existed apart from the place where so much of their past was contained.

After ordering their meal, Grey reached out and captured her hand across the table. "We've spent most of our time over the past two weeks talking about Land's End and what needs to be done." He stroked his thumbs over the lines of her palm. "For the remainder of today, it would be nice if we wouldn't mention the boardwalk or any of its people."

"Okay," she agreed easily. "Then tell me about your years in New York City." She removed her hand from his as the waitress appeared with their drink orders and salads.

"There isn't much to tell about those years," Grey said when the waitress had disappeared, leaving them alone. "I worked long hours six days a week. Sunday was the only day I could truly call mine."

"And what did you do on those days off?"

"First thing after getting up, I'd walk to a nearby deli where they had fresh-baked blueberry bagels and the best coffee I've ever tasted. On most afternoons, I went to a matinee at one of the theaters, then spent the evenings sitting on my balcony breathing in the smog and watching the world go by." He shrugged and smiled. "Pretty benign stuff."

What he didn't tell her was how often on those Sunday afternoons his thoughts had turned to her. How often he'd wondered what she was doing, who she was doing it with, if she ever thought of him. "Anyway," he continued, "I felt like I was just half-alive until I came back here. This will always be home."

She nodded. "I know what you mean. I thought about leaving here after Johnny left and . . . everything."

"Where did you think about going?" he asked.

"Bridget and Lars own a cabin a couple of hours from here. It's isolated and rather primitive, but at that time in my life I thought I'd make a very fine hermit."

Grey laughed. "Oh, Nikki, if there's anyone less likely to become a hermit, I don't know who it would be."

She grinned her agreement. "That's what I decided. I couldn't stand the thought of not running next door to have coffee with Bridget and not hearing the laughter of the kids who come to the puppet shows. Talking to trees and overgrown brush just doesn't hold the same appeal as talking with people."

Once again, he reached across the table and captured her hand in his. "I'm glad you didn't leave. I can't imagine the boardwalk without you."

"And I can't imagine myself without the boardwalk."

He squeezed her hand, enjoying the way the candlelight danced in the depths of her hazel eyes. It gave them a green-blue luster, like the color of the ocean on a cloudy day. "I hope nothing ever happens to you again that makes you think you need to escape and become a hermit."

"It won't." She shook her hair away from her face and raised her chin defiantly. "I'll never let it."

"I asked you this question before and you told me it was none of my business, but I'd really like to know. Did you love your husband?"

Again Nikki took her hand from his, her thoughts obviously back in time. She frowned and reached for a strand of her hair, which she worried and twisted between two fingers. "I loved what Johnny did for me. I was frightened and felt foolish and unwanted, and he picked me up and soothed my fears and made me believe, no matter what, it would all be okay. But if you're asking me if I was in love with him, no, I wasn't. Nor was he with me. We were good friends...still are good friends."

Grey frowned, surprised at how envious he was of a man he'd never met. Johnny had been there through Nikki's pregnancy. He'd seen her body ripening and glowing with growing life. He'd experienced everything that by rights should have belonged to Grey. I should hate him, Grey thought, surprised to find he didn't. He envied him, but also was thankful that he was there for Nikki when Grey himself could not be.

Grey thought of the little baby girl—*his* little baby girl. Pain ripped through him at the thought. Like a quick jab to the midsection, it momentarily stole his breath away. He should have been there to hold Nikki. He should have been there to say goodbye to the child their love had created. He consciously fought against the image, unable to face the tormenting, overwhelming sadness.

"Where is Johnny now?" he asked, taking a sip of his wine in an effort to wash down the lump in his throat.

"Who knows?" She smiled softly, and the softness of that smile made Grey's heart ache with a strange kind of hurt. "Johnny blows with the wind. About once a month I get a letter from him, always from a different place, always detailing his vagabond life-style." She hesitated, as if about to say something, then picked up her wineglass, instead. "Anyway, Johnny is a fond part of my past."

"And what am I?" Grey asked lightly, but as the silence stretched and he waited for her answer, he found his heart pounding an unsteady rhythm of anticipation. He suddenly realized how important her answer was to him.

She looked at him, her hazel eyes darkened with confusion and some undefinable emotion. "I don't know, Grey. I honestly don't know."

Eight

———

Nikki stood before the floor-length mirror on the back of her bedroom door, staring at the reflected image. Nikki Young had disappeared and the woman who stared back at her was a stranger.

She looked chic, sophisticated, a far cry from the waif with the untamed hair and cutoff shorts who roamed the boardwalk.

It's the dress, she decided as she studied her reflection. The sleek black material bared her shoulders and clung to her curves. It made her feel feminine and sexy. Or perhaps it's the hair, she thought. She considered the dark tresses, neatly confined in the French braid.

No, it wasn't any one thing that made her look different. It was a combination of things—the dress, the hairstyle and probably most of all the nervous energy that caused butterflies to dance a frenzied rhythm in her stomach. It's silly to be nervous, she chided herself. It's just a dinner party. But she knew in truth it was more than that. For most of her relationship with Grey, both past and present, they had been in her world. They'd spent all their time, ate most of their meals at the boardwalk.

Tonight, for the very first time, she was entering his world. It suddenly seemed very important that she show him she could be a part of that world, where unspoken rules of behavior prevailed.

She moved away from the mirror and stepped into the high-heel black pumps, unable to remember the last time she'd worn them. Had she worn them for her wedding? Funny, she wasn't sure.

She turned around as the door to her bedroom opened. She smiled nervously as Bridget peeked in. "Ah, sweetheart, you look beautiful." She stepped inside the bedroom and walked toward Nikki. "Here...sit down," she instructed, pointing to the bed.

Nikki sat down and Bridget pulled a necklace out of her pocket and fastened it around Nikki's neck.

When Bridget was finished, Nikki looked down at the golden locket that nestled between her breasts, then looked at her friend questioningly.

"It was your mother's." Bridget sat down next to Nikki on the bed. "She gave it to me to keep for you. She wanted you to have it for a very special occasion and I can't think of anything more special than tonight's effort to save the boardwalk."

Nikki opened the locket and looked at the pictures inside. On one side was a photo of her mother, and on the other was one of Nikki at the age of three.

Bridget touched her arm lightly. "I was going to give it to you years ago." Her smile was soft, filled with a hint of sorrow. "I wanted to give it to you when Lolly was born, but..." She shrugged and patted Nikki's arm. "Anyway, it just seems like the right time now."

Nikki closed the locket and clasped it in one hand, the gold warm against her skin. She fought against the pain that was always there, so close, so eager to be acknowledged.

She closed her eyes and took a deep breath, relieved when she felt the wave of sorrow ebb, leaving a dull ache she'd long ago learned to live with.

She leaned over and gave Bridget a warm hug. "Thanks," she said, surprised at the huskiness of emotion still rife in her voice. She stood up and did a quick pirouette. "So you really think I look all right?"

"More than all right." Bridget's smile was filled with a maternal pride. "You look more beautiful than I've ever seen you look. Are you nervous?"

"A little," Nikki admitted with a wry grin. "I'm not accustomed to rubbing elbows with the elite of Oceanview." Her smile faded. "But I know how important this night is to Grey and Land's End."

"But Grey's already made a commitment to keep the boardwalk open."

Nikki nodded. "But it's a commitment he'll find difficult to keep without the financial support of the Oceanview merchants."

"Oh, pooh, the Blakemores have more money than Midas himself," Bridget scoffed.

"Perhaps, but I don't think the Blakemore money can subsidize the boardwalk indefinitely. There needs to be long-term, permanent changes to assure that Land's End will grow and prosper." She smiled sheepishly, realizing she sounded as if she were on a soapbox. "Grey and I have come up with some very definite plans, but we need the assistance of the people of Oceanview. All we have to do is convince those people that helping Land's End is in their best interest."

"Honey, in that dress, you could convince a polar bear to move to Africa." Bridget jumped off the bed. "And now I'd better get back next door. Lars will be trying to make his own dinner and is liable to burn down the whole house without me there to supervise." She stood on tiptoe and gave Nikki a quick hug. "Now don't you be nervous. You just be yourself and show all those stuffy townspeople what we're made of out here."

"I'll do the best I can for all of us," Nikki said, then jumped as a knock sounded on her front door. She looked at the alarm clock on the dresser and took a deep breath. "That will be Grey."

Together the two women left the bedroom. Bridget opened the door and greeted Grey. "My, don't you look spiffy," she observed as he walked in.

Nikki felt her heart catch in her chest as she gazed at him. Spiffy? No, that didn't even begin to describe how Grey looked. He looked wonderfully virile, magnificently handsome. His black suit jacket fit his broad shoulders perfectly and tapered to emphasize his slender waist. His slacks hugged the length of his legs and were obviously tailored specifically for him. His crisp white shirt was silk, merely adding to his masculinity.

But what kept her breath uneven was the flare of emotion that sparked in his eyes as his gaze lingered on her. Heated passion, fiery want lit their depths and Nikki felt an answering need warm her deep inside. It was amazing how he could make her tremble with a mere glance.

"You look...stunning," he murmured softly.

Nikki smiled shakily and ran her hands self-consciously down the sides of her dress. "I'll bet you say that to all the girls."

He shook his head, his eyes deepening in hue. "No. Only you."

"Well, I think I'll leave you two to your mutual admiration society," Bridget interjected, grinning at both of them. "Have fun, you two, and give 'em hell."

Grey laughed. "We will."

Within minutes, Bridget disappeared back to her house and Nikki and Grey were in his car driving the short distance to the Blakemore house.

As he drove, Nikki studied him, smiling as he caught her scrutinizing him. "What are you looking at?" He asked indulgently.

"Your gray hair. I noticed it that night when you first came to the theater. You're only twenty-five years old...far too young to have these silver hairs." She reached across the seat and gently touched the tinsel-colored strands among the dark ones above his ears. "And it's positively sinful that it looks so wonderful on you."

"My father was completely silver-haired by the time he was thirty." He touched his temple self-consciously, then turned and gazed at her, his eyes once again holding the white heat that momentarily stole her breath away. "You know what gave me these gray hairs?"

She shook her head, caught in the haze of passion that shadowed his eyes and burned her soul.

"Living without you for seven years. Loss turned my hair gray and stole my dreams away from me."

"Grey..." Nikki sighed softly in protest. She didn't want to hear this, not now, not with her nerves taut in anticipation of the party and her heart still surrounded by a shield of protection. There was still a piece of herself she was afraid to surrender to him.

"Okay, I won't say any more for now," he said quietly. "But sooner or later, Nikki, we've got to figure out where we're going with each other. I've been patient, but before long, my patience will reach an end."

"Later," she murmured. "All I want to concentrate on tonight is saving the boardwalk."

He reached out and captured her hand in his. "Okay, tonight we concentrate on the boardwalk, but eventually you're going to have to concentrate on us."

"Eventually," she agreed vaguely, the nervous butterflies once again taking wing in the pit of her stomach as Grey parked in front of the Blakemore house.

As they walked up the walkway that led to the huge, stone mansion, Nikki remembered all the times she'd stood in the distance on the beach and looked up toward this house and wondered what Grey was doing.

In her youthful imaginings, she'd thought of Grey as a young prince, trapped in the huge cold houseful of collectibles and antiques. He'd been the poor little rich boy, imprisoned by society's mores, trapped by family expectations and responsibilities. And she'd been certain only her love could save him.

She'd hated this house and all that it represented, but now she realized it was nothing more than stone and wood. It and the people inside could no longer hurt her. They no longer had the power to touch her at all. Thomas Blakemore had given it his best shot, and she had survived. And no matter what happened between her and Grey this time around, she would survive.

As Grey opened the front door to allow her entry, she straightened her shoulders and lifted her chin. Bridget was right. The best thing for her to do was be herself and let the chips fall where they may. One way or another, the issue of the boardwalk would be settled this evening. And then she was going to have to figure out exactly how she felt about Grey.

The living room was filled with people clumped together in small groups throughout the massive area. Nikki recognized most of them, having seen them in town or with their families on the boardwalk several times each summer.

She tensed as she saw Grey's mother break away from one of the groups and approach where she and Grey stood. Nikki hadn't seen Mrs. Blakemore for years, not since that fateful summer when Grey had gone to college and disappeared from Nikki's life.

As she walked across the floor, Nikki observed that the passing years had not been as kind to her as they had been to her son. Her face was deeply lined and she was thinner, smaller than Nikki remembered.

"Nikki." She reached out and took Nikki's hands in hers. "I'm so glad you could come this evening."

"Thank you for opening your home for this particular purpose," Nikki replied, removing her hands from the older woman's grasp. A surge of bitterness rose inside as she thought of Grey's mother's part in her husband's duplicity.

"Grey, why don't you go get something for Nikki to drink?" Mrs. Blakemore suggested.

"White wine?" Grey asked.

Nikki nodded her assent and Grey left the two women alone. Once again Mrs. Blakemore reached out and took Nikki's hands. "I've thought of you often over the years," she said, her voice trembling with deep emotion. She sighed, and to Nikki's surprise the older woman's eyes misted with tears. "I know you will probably never forgive me . . . can never forgive me for what my husband did to you and Grey, but I just wanted you to know that I'm sorry I wasn't strong enough to take control and change things. I live with that regret every day of my life."

Nikki tried to hang on to the bitterness that had always shielded her. However, as she felt the trembling in the older woman's hand, saw the grief that darkened her blue eyes, she felt her bitterness crystalize and shatter and fall away from her heart. "It's all in the past and it's time we started fresh and put that past behind us."

Mrs. Blakemore gave Nikki's hands a last squeeze, then released them. She hesitated a moment. "I go to the cemetery, you know," she said softly, her gaze not quite meeting Nikki's. "I go there often and sit and talk to the little girl who would have been my granddaughter." Pain, ripe and vivid etched Mrs. Blakemore's face, making her wrinkles deepen.

For a moment, Nikki was so surprised, she couldn't speak. Somehow, knowing Grey's mother shared her grief made it easier for Nikki to forgive. Nikki's throat filled with thick emotion and she swallowed hard around it. "She was a beautiful little girl," she finally said softly. "I like to imagine her cradled in angel wings with a chorus of heavenly voices singing her lullabies each night.''

"Oh, how beautiful." Grey's mother's eyes shone brightly and Nikki knew Mrs. Blakemore was imagining her baby granddaughter in the loving arms of angels. She smiled at Nikki and for a single moment a connection was forged between the two women, a connection that found its strength in shared grief and love.

"Here we are." Grey rejoined them and handed Nikki a glass of wine.

"Well, I'd better go check on dinner. You two go on and mingle with the others." Mrs. Blakemore gave Nikki another lingering smile, then turned and walked away.

"You okay?" Grey asked Nikki, touching her arm in concern.

"Fine," Nikki said, flashing him a reassuring smile.

"Come on." Grey placed one hand at Nikki's elbow. "I'll introduce you to everyone."

For the next hour, Grey introduced Nikki to all the people in the room. The majority of the guests were the Oceanview merchants, but there were family friends present, as well.

The predinner conversation was light and pleasant and Nikki found herself slowly relaxing. Suddenly, she realized these people were no different from the ones on the boardwalk. They had the same dreams, the same need for love and a sense of belonging. They spilled their wine, talked too loudly and had their own set of peccadilloes that made them nothing more, nothing less than human.

By the time dinner was served and the conversation turned to Land's End, Nikki felt comfortable enough to champion the area that was her home and the people who were her friends.

She spoke from her heart, warmed by Grey's gaze. She shared her vision for the boardwalk's future and her concerns on how the closing of the boardwalk might affect Oceanview.

Over coffee and dessert, Grey told all the merchants what sort of financial commitment he'd like from each of them. He answered their questions and spoke again of the consequences to the town of Oceanview should the boardwalk close down.

By the time dessert was finished, Grey had received what he wanted from the merchants of Oceanview, and Nikki knew with the town and the people of the boardwalk working together, Land's End would be around a long time to entertain local families and tourists.

It was nearly eleven o'clock when Nikki and Grey stood at the front door, thanking everyone and telling them goodbye. "Amanda, thank you for coming," Grey said to the tall blond woman who was in the process of leaving.

"I thought I should be here since my father couldn't be," she said.

"Amanda's father owns the Oceanview newspaper," Grey explained to Nikki.

Amanda smiled thinly, her gaze cool as it lingered on Nikki. "And I understand you run the puppet theater."

"Yes, I do."

"Nikki is extremely talented," Grey said, smiling as he placed an arm around Nikki's shoulders.

"Oh, I'm sure she is," Amanda replied. "I'm sure she must have many hidden talents." Despite her pleasant smile, she obviously meant her tone to be insulting.

"If you'll excuse me, I'll just go and see if there's anything I can do to help your mother." Blatantly ignoring Amanda, Nikki turned and left the two standing at the door.

"I can't believe I was so rude." Nikki giggled as she remembered the indignant look on Amanda's face. She reached up and worked with her fingers to loosen her hair from the confining braid. She'd insisted Grey put the top down on his car before he drove her home. She wanted to feel the night wind, blowing away the memory of Amanda's snide look.

"She deserved it," Grey observed, grinning at her as he loosened his tie and pulled it off. He drove slowly, dividing his attention between the road and Nikki.

He felt a tightening in his groin as she released her hair from its imprisoning braid and it swirled around her head like a cloud of rich darkness.

He'd watched her all night, wanting her, needing her. In the sleek black dress, with her hair neat and restrained, she'd seemed distant and untouchable. He'd wanted to lay her down on the floor and rip the dress off her. He'd wanted to loosen her hair, tangle his hands in it and kiss her lips until they were swollen and red.

Now that the issue of the boardwalk was settled, he wanted them to focus exclusively on where they were going with their relationship. With this thought in mind, he exited the main road and drove across the sand toward the shoreline. He wanted to walk along the beach with her, make wishes upon stars, make love beneath the moon's full illumination.

He parked the car and turned to her. "How about a walk along the beach?"

She nodded, her eyes gleaming with promise, as if she knew his need because it was hers, as well. He got out of the car and pulled off his shoes and socks, then waited a moment as she kicked off her high heels and removed her panty hose.

When she got out of the car, he reached for her hand and together they walked slowly up the beach.

The moon was bright overhead, dancing in the darkness of her hair and highlighting the structure of her face. She seemed to glow, as if her body drank in the moonlight and reflected it from her pores.

Again, Grey felt his body's response to her. She was the strongest aphrodisiac he'd ever known. Just looking at her could make him hard and hungry. But he knew it was more than her physical beauty that attracted him. Her spirit called to his, filling him with everything he needed to exist.

She turned and gazed at him, a small smile curving her lips upward. "You should be feeling very proud of yourself. You did a wonderful job in presenting the problems of the boardwalk tonight."

"Let's just hope the solution works. I don't want them to go home and forget all the reasons for helping Land's End."

"They won't, and it will work." She hesitated a moment, then continued, "You have a way of making people believe in what you believe. It's always been one of your strongest gifts."

"I know you once believed in me...." Grey hesitated, his emotion thick in his throat. He turned and took her by the shoulders, his hands caressing the smooth tanned flesh. He noted the sun freckles that dotted her shoulders and fought the desire to lean over and kiss each one. He wanted to know what she felt, needed to know what thoughts twirled around her head concerning him. At that moment, he needed that more than he needed to make love to her. "Can you ever believe in me again, Nikki?"

Her eyes glittered in the moonlight, wide and tumultuous as the water that crashed to the sandy beach. She turned her head and gazed out toward the ocean, releasing a sigh as strong as the night wind that ruffled her hair. "I believe... I want a swim."

With a quicksilver move, she shrugged out of her dress and underclothes and ran for the water, never looking back to where Grey stood on the shore.

He watched her as she dived into the waves, her slender body painted with the moon's silver light. He sighed with a tinge of disappointment.

She wasn't ready. For some reason or other, there was a gulf between them he didn't understand, couldn't begin to comprehend.

For the past several weeks, they had worked side by side, laughing together and sharing with each other. They had made love with the same intensity, found the same kind of glory in each other's arms that they'd had years before.

So, what was wrong? There were times when he felt her gaze on him, expectant... as if she anticipated something he would say or do. But he didn't know what she wanted, what she needed from him, and somehow he felt as if he disappointed her in some way.

He stared off at the distant stars, wishing he knew the workings of her mind. What was it she wanted from him? What was it she needed from him? He'd turn himself inside out to please her. But, whatever it was that kept her distant, it was something she wasn't ready to discuss, something she didn't want to admit.

Why did he feel as if he wasn't getting to the core of Nikki, the hidden place that held her trust, her dreams, her forevers? She'd allowed him in seven years ago, and he'd found it a place that filled him with shimmering light and love.

Had that merely been the intensity of first love? No. He turned his gaze back to her, a silver mermaid riding the moon-kissed waves. No, it was much more complex than the bittersweet memory of a first love. What he felt were the emotions of a grown man, a man who knew exactly what he wanted for himself.

He knew with certainty that he wanted to get into that secret guarded place again. He wanted Nikki's trust, he wanted her dreams. And more than ever, he wanted her forevers. Now all he had to figure out was how to make her want the same thing from him.

Nine

Nikki set her paintbrush aside and climbed down the ladder where she'd been standing for the last hour. She walked over to a nearby bench and sat down. Bunching her hair up, she allowed the light morning breeze to cool the back of her neck. She closed her eyes and leaned her head against the hard wood of the bench.

"Nikki, you all right?"

She opened her eyes as Bridget sat down next to her. She smiled at the woman, noting the streak of brilliant blue paint that decorated the side of her nose. "I'm fine. I just needed to take a little break."

She released her hold on her hair, allowing it to tumble down her back. A smile curved her lips as she looked around. Activity was taking place everywhere, and in the past three weeks the boardwalk had begun its transformation. "It's looking good, isn't it," she observed.

Bridget nodded. "It's beginning to look like it did when I first came here years ago—all sparkling and new, full of dreams and magic."

Yes, Nikki thought, the boardwalk looked new and sparkling, but somewhere in the past seven years she had lost the magic and she didn't think it would ever return for her. She sighed wearily and pulled her hair up once again.

"Are you sure you're feeling all right?" Bridget asked, her gaze probing as it lingered on Nikki.

Nikki nodded. "I'm just tired, that's all."

"You've been tired a lot lately."

"I've been working hard."

"Speaking of working hard, where's Grey this morning?" Bridget asked curiously.

"He was meeting with the printer this morning to check over the brochures and publicity mailers."

Bridget clapped her hands together in excitement. "With all the publicity he's generating, these walkways should be filled with people every day and night.''

"We might not see a big change for the rest of this summer, but by next summer business should really pick up.''

"Speaking of picking up, I'd better pick up my butt and get back to work.'' Bridget jumped off the bench and observed Nikki once again. "You know, it wouldn't hurt for you to go to the doctor and get a checkup. You've looked pale for the last couple of days.'' She paused a moment, a hopeful smile lighting her face. "You don't think you might be pregnant, do you?''

"Don't be ridiculous,'' Nikki scoffed, ignoring the small jab of pain that pierced her heart. "You know that's impossible.''

"You told me forgiving Grey was impossible,'' Bridget said.

"Different kinds of impossible,'' Nikki said laughingly. She watched as Bridget returned to painting an area of replaced railing. In the distance, a group of men worked to install a portion of new walkway, while another crew removed burned-out bulbs in the strings of colored lights on the Ferris wheel.

In the past three weeks, Grey's plans for rejuvenation had come to pass. The Oceanview hardware store had donated paint, the printing shop was donating the material and printing of flyers and brochures that the chamber of commerce would mail out around the country. Other shops and boutiques were donating to the boardwalk a portion of their profits from the sale of Land's End souvenirs.

There was a new community feel, a pleasant, equitable merging of the town and the boardwalk that had never been present before. Even the teenagers were getting into the act, donating their time to help in the work taking place. Yes, everything was coming together nicely...everything except her relationship with Grey.

She frowned and closed her eyes once again, her mind instantly creating a mental picture of Grey. That night after the party, they had made love on the beach and it had been as glorious, as wonderful as ever. The physical side of the relationship with Grey was easy, always had been easy. Physically, they were perfectly attuned, two halves of a whole.

The emotional side was less clear-cut, more difficult to figure out. She loved Grey, knew now that she had never completely stopped loving him. She'd resolved the fact that he'd had nothing to do with the events that had torn them apart so long ago.

The bitterness that had always wrapped itself around her heart and shielded her was gone, dissipated by the sheer strength of his touch, his kiss, his smile, his very presence in her life.

And yet, she released another tired sigh and frowned, trying to figure out what it was that held her heart captive, why there was a piece of herself trapped deep inside where he couldn't touch it. There was a portion of the special magic gone between them . . . and it was this missing piece that made it impossible for her to commit to him completely.

She dropped her hair once again and leaned forward, willing her body to get up and go back to work. For the past week, she'd fought off an overwhelming exhaustion that had made every physical act seem impossible.

"Maybe Bridget is right and I should go in for a checkup," she muttered as she stood up. She'd had mononucleosis several years ago and wondered if perhaps she was having a relapse.

Climbing the ladder, she started to paint the front of the puppet theater. She'd worked for about an hour when she saw Grey approaching.

As always, at the sight of him clad in his cutoff jeans and T-shirt, her heart danced an unsteady rhythm. Over the past couple of weeks, he'd tanned to a deep bronze color that emphasized the chiseled lines of his face and gave him an outdoorsy, heathy appearance.

"It's looking good," he said from the bottom of the ladder. His eyes twinkled and she realized he wasn't speaking of the newly painted theater, but rather of his view of her jean-clad derriere on the ladder above where he stood.

"You're incorrigible." She laughed and descended to stand beside him.

"Better to be incorrigible than incompetent," he observed, his eyes speaking of silk sheets and sweet abandon as they gazed at her.

"Oh, you're definitely more than competent," she replied, feeling a hot lick of response ignite in her veins. How easily he could make all their surroundings disappear and make her think only of being in his arms.

She consciously shoved aside the images his gaze evoked. Now was not the time or the place to follow through on the passion for him that was always a mere heartbeat away. "So, what do you think?" She gestured toward the freshly painted facade of the theater.

Grey studied it, nodding his head in approval. "I like it. The orange and yellow will definitely catch the eyes of the kids. It looks like a bright sun wearing a big orange hat."

Nikki smiled at his fanciful image. He'd changed in the weeks since his return to the boardwalk. Slowly but surely, the enchantment of Land's End was getting to him. "And when I finish painting the window shutters orange, it will look like the sun has orange eyebrows."

He laughed. "Just like yours," he replied, taking a finger and tracing the curve of one of her eyebrows. "You have orange and yellow speckles all over your face."

"It will wash," she said. She pointed to the papers he held. "What have you got?"

He handed her a slick, folded brochure. "Behold the wonder of Land's End."

Nikki took the brochure and opened it, gazing in pleasure at the advertisement of her home. In professionally produced photos, the boardwalk was depicted in all its glory. "Oh, Grey," she gasped in delight, "these are terrific."

"And beginning tomorrow, they'll be mailed all over the country. Land's End is going to live, Nikki. It's going to survive and be around a very long time."

Nikki threw her arms around him, loving him not only for the way he made her feel, but for what he had done to help the boardwalk.

He immediately responded to her, wrapping his arms around her and holding her tight against the length of his body. "Hmm, I should bring you brochures more often," he said, his breath warm and tantalizing in her ear. He released her reluctantly. "Unfortunately, I came bearing bad news, as well."

"What?" Nikki stepped away from him to concentrate completely on what he said.

"I've got to catch an afternoon flight to New York. There's a crisis in the office and it seems I'm the only one who can solve it."

"How long will you be gone?" She would miss him . . . a lot. She felt the echo of a past hurt . . . the memory of holding him, loving him just before he left for college. She shook her head to dispel the memory.

He shrugged. "Who knows. As long as it takes to straighten out the mess. A couple of days, perhaps a week." He pulled her into his arms again, his chin resting atop her hair. "Will you miss me?" he murmured softly.

"Perhaps a little," she admitted, smiling as his hands rubbed languidly across the small of her back. "Maybe more than a little," she added, molding herself to his body warmth and masculine form.

"I'm going to miss you," he whispered, his voice deeper than usual. "I'm going to miss you like hell." He moved his hand up and stroked the length of her hair. "Nikki, when I get back, I want to talk to you about our future."

"Oh, Grey, can't we just take it one day at a time?" she protested, a dull dread coursing swiftly through her.

"We *have* been taking it one day at a time, but now I want to look beyond today, beyond tomorrow. Nikki. . . ." He broke away from her and sighed in frustration. "I can't get into it now. I've got to be at the airport in an hour, but we'll talk when I get back, okay?" He looked at her. "Okay?" he pressed.

She nodded. He smiled, touched a finger to the tip of her nose, then leaned forward and kissed her soundly on the lips. "I'll call you when I can." With this, he turned and hurried off in the direction of his car.

Nikki watched him go, loving him as much as she had ever loved anyone. But was it enough? What was it that made her hesitate where he was concerned? What was it that made her afraid to commit to him in the way she had committed when she was seventeen?

She no longer blamed him for leaving her, no longer felt any bitterness about the past. So why did she feel a part of herself holding back? What was the nebulous struggle going on inside her head? She didn't know. But she had until Grey returned to Land's End to find the answer.

She climbed back up the ladder, but instead of returning to her work, she retrieved her paint and brush and decided to call it a day. She was tired, overwhelmingly so, and all she wanted to do was go home and take a long nap. She'd paint later, just as she'd think about Grey later, when she was rested and things didn't seem so muddled in her mind.

* * *

"So, am I going to live?" Nikki asked.

Dr. Vendricks smiled at her and gestured for her to sit in the chair across from his desk.

Nikki sat down, completely at ease with the white-haired man who'd been her physician since she'd been a small child. It had been Dr. Vendricks who had doctored her childhood measles, taken out her tonsils, treated her bout of mono and delivered Lolly.

"It should just be a few minutes and we'll have the last of the test results," he explained. She nodded and waited patiently as he bent over her chart and made several notations.

As always when sitting quietly, her thoughts went directly to Grey. He'd been in New York for a week. A week in which she had missed him desperately, frantically...frighteningly. She hadn't realized what an integral part of her life he'd come to be until this past week, nor had she managed to figure out why she had a horrible dread that somehow she and Grey weren't destined to be forever, that the dreams of forever they'd once had would remain forever only in their dreams.

He'd called every night, silly phone calls filled with inane conversation, small talk just to connect, just to hear each other's voices. Each night when Nikki had hung up, she'd wondered what it was that made her feel empty inside, as if there was a desperate need he didn't, couldn't ever fill. It was infuriating, to know that something was wrong, yet be unable to identify the source.

Nikki started as knuckles rapped on the door, followed by Nurse Kelly peeking her head inside. "The last of the results," she said. She stepped inside and handed the papers to Dr. Vendricks, then left, closing the door behind her.

"Just as I thought." Dr. Vendricks shoved his eyeglasses atop his head and leaned back in his chair.

"It's . . . it's nothing serious, is it?" Nikki asked.

"Nothing that a little time won't take care of." He paused a moment, a smile turning up the sides of his white mustache. "Nikki, you're pregnant."

She stared at him, not moving for a moment, not breathing as his words pierced the veil of disbelief that surrounded her. "But . . . but you told me years ago that it would be impossible for me to get pregnant again," she finally managed to sputter.

Dr. Vendricks smiled and templed his hands beneath his chin. "My dear, I believe what I told you was that it would be *nearly* impossible, that it would take a small miracle." His smile widened. "And it looks like you found your miracle."

A miracle? Minutes later, Nikki sat numbly in her car, staring at the dashboard in a haze of disbelief. Pregnant. She was pregnant. Her hand fell to her stomach, still flat, not showing any outward sign of

the life that grew inside. A baby...her baby...
Grey's baby. The words spun in her head in nau-
seating, dizzying fashion until she slumped forward and rested her forehead on the steering wheel.

It's like history repeating itself, she thought in
despair. She suddenly felt achingly young and ter-
rifyingly alone. As she sat there, rubbing her stomach, thinking of the past...the future...the baby
she now carried and the baby she had lost, she suddenly realized what was wrong between her and
Grey.

With an overwhelming sense of anguish, she understood that she and Grey could never have a forever together. And she knew with a certainty that
once again she would be pregnant alone. He hadn't
been able to share the grief, the memory of their
first child with her, and that was something she
could never forgive.

Grey raced across the sand toward the boardwalk, his long legs carrying him quickly across the
morning-cool sand. He'd taken a red-eye from New
York and arrived at home only minutes before, long
enough to get out of his business suit and into a pair
of shorts.

The past week in the city had seemed intermina-
ble, filled with crises and headaches, meetings and
stress. He'd missed the scent of the ocean, the

bright lights of the boardwalk. But most of all, he'd missed Nikki. His need to be with her wrapped around him, entangled inside him, making it the most powerful need he'd ever experienced.

His footsteps thundered down the wooden walkway toward her house. It was still so early, she wouldn't have left for the pizza place yet.

He wanted to wake her up, caress her sleep-warmed body, watch as the lingering traces of sleepiness were replaced by the fires of passion. He wanted to capture her soft, mewling morning sounds in the hollow of his neck, feel her body mold itself against his.

Rapidly he knocked on her door, the sharp raps breaking through the stillness of the early morning. He paused, imagining her hazel eyes fluttering open, her long golden legs swinging over the edge of the bed, her hand reaching for her robe so she could come to the door. "Nikki, it's me," he yelled, hoping she would dispense with the robe and meet him in her sweet-smelling skin and nothing else.

When she opened the door, he didn't even care that she was already dressed. For a moment, he merely stood, smiling like a damn fool, drinking in the sight of her.

She wore a pair of jean shorts and a red blouse that exposed her tanned midsection. As usual, her hair tumbled wildly down her back. He loved every riotous curl.

It wasn't until he gazed in her eyes that he realized something was wrong. Her eyes held an emptiness. The same dull emptiness that had darkened them on the night she had told him about Lolly was there again, changing the hazel hue to the shade of a muddied stream. "Nikki...is something wrong?"

"Come in." She opened the door to allow him entry. "When did you get back?"

"Just a little while ago. I changed clothes and came right over." He wanted to touch her, needed to hug her, kiss her, but there was a distance in her eyes, a distance that warned him off, a distance that made him afraid. "Nikki, what's going on? Did something happen while I was away?"

She shook her head and motioned for him to sit down on the vibrant-colored sofa. Grey hesitated, his heart thudding a dull dread. Finally, he sat down and looked at her expectantly.

For a long moment, she didn't say anything. Obviously distracted and nervous, she walked around the room, her gaze not meeting his. "I've been doing a lot of thinking this past week, Grey," she finally said.

"You know that's always dangerous." He offered her a grin, then quickly inverted it when she didn't respond. What was happening here? He felt as if he'd drifted into a movie theater halfway through the screening and was desperately trying to catch up with the plot. "Nikki, for God's sake, what's going on?"

She drew a hand across her forehead. It trembled as it came to rest on the little wrinkle that appeared just over her left eye whenever she frowned.

She drew in a deep breath, released it with a tremor, then dropped her hand to her side and looked at him. "Grey, I thought we could pick up where we'd left off so many years ago. When I found out that you hadn't let me down, hadn't left me pregnant and alone, I thought we could get back some of the magic we once shared . . . but I know now I was wrong."

"What are you talking about?" He stared at her in disbelief.

She looked off to the side, apparently unable to meet the intensity of his gaze. She laughed, an empty sound that rang untrue. "I've never been able to think very well when you're around. Since you've been away in New York, I've done nothing but think." She sighed once again. "We can't go back and recapture what we once had . . . it's been tainted, ruined. Too much time has passed, too much bitterness is still inside me. I can't let go. I can't love you again."

He stood up and in three strides crossed to where she stood. He placed his hands on her shoulders, looking deep into her eyes . . . eyes shuttered to the intrusion, darkened with emotion he couldn't fathom. "But you do love me," he said softly. "I know you do, Nikki. I feel it every time you're in my arms, every time we make love."

She twisted away from him and stepped back. "You feel passion, Grey...and desire. I won't deny that sex has always been incredible with you." She raised her chin and eyed him defiantly. "I'm as healthy as the next person. I like good sex, but that doesn't mean I love you. I think we've been confusing the two."

For a moment, Grey couldn't speak. He was stunned by her words, appalled by her demeaning what they had, turning it into nothing more than lust. "Nikki, lust doesn't last for seven years. Love does," he observed. "I love you, Nikki."

"Don't talk to me about love, Grey." Her anger came at him from nowhere, with no warning signals, no buildup. He saw the flash of fire in her eyes, felt the tension that rolled off her as she faced him.

He stepped back from her, momentarily dazed by the strength of her anger, the bitterness that glittered harshly in her eyes. "You've never asked me a single question. I've waited...hoped...needed you to talk to me." She stalked across the room, away from him, but her angry glittering gaze didn't leave his face. "Ever since the night I told you about the baby, I've waited for you to talk to me, ask me about her, but you've never even mentioned her name to me. . . ." The words ended on a sob.

Lolly. Her name rose in his mind, bringing with it the grief that threatened to plunge him into a darkness so profound, he feared he'd never find the light again. He fought against it, didn't want it, wasn't ready to deal with it.

He stared at her, wanting to say something . . . knowing he needed to say something, but the lump in his throat was too large to speak around. It threatened to strangle him, forced him to stare at her in helpless confusion.

"Let me go, Grey," she said softly, her tears sparkling like dewdrops in the morning sunshine streaking through the window. "Let *us* go. I need you to be in my past."

It hurt. He hurt and he couldn't think. Emotions balled up inside him, confusing him. He loved her. He didn't want to let her go. He loved her, recognized her pain and knew he must let her go. "Nikki . . ." He cleared his throat, then continued, "Are you sure?"

She wrapped her arms around herself, shivered slightly, but when she looked at him, her gaze was steady, still holding the lingering darkness of intense anger. "I'm sure," she said firmly.

With a vague nod of his head, Grey turned and left the house. When he was gone, Nikki stumbled over to the sofa and sank onto it, unable to control the shivering that suffused her body.

Finally... finally after seven years, there was closure. She and Grey had finally managed to close the book on their relationship. It was over. Finished.

After leaving the doctor's office the day before, Nikki had realized that since the night on the beach when she had told him about Lolly, she'd been waiting for him to talk to her, grieve with her. The morning she'd stumbled upon him at the gravesite and they'd made love, she'd thought she'd felt a piece of his grief. She'd waited for him to follow up on it, needing him to ask about the child they had lost.

Each and every moment they'd spent together, she'd anticipated his questions, his need to know about the little girl, his need to share the full brunt of his grief with her. And each time she'd been disappointed. She hadn't comprehended that the endless disappointment was creating a ball of bitterness inside her, a wall he would never succeed in breaching.

She'd suddenly realized the day before that he would never give her what she needed most because he didn't feel it the way she did. He hadn't been there. He hadn't gone through it. He had no grief. To him, it was a distant tragedy that didn't touch him, didn't haunt him.

It was at that moment she'd realized there was no hope for a future between them. Her grief was the last piece of herself she selfishly guarded, the piece that would forever keep her distant from Grey.

She clasped the locket that hung around her neck. It should have held her picture...Lolly's picture. Nikki gasped back a sob.

How could she love again when her heart was still so heavy with grief? And how could she love a man who didn't grieve?

Yes, she'd done the right thing in closing the door on her relationship with Grey. Hopefully, he'd drift away from the boardwalk, go back to the Blakemore business interests in New York City. He'd forget about her and never know about this new baby. Yes, she had done the right thing and all would be fine just as soon as she stopped crying.

Ten

It took two days for Grey to get angry. Initially, he'd left her house and run along the beach, trying to outrace the memory of her anger, her bitterness, and trying to shove aside the haunting, suffocating thoughts of the little girl he'd never seen, never held.

Maybe it was time to put it all in the past, he'd finally conceded. They'd sorted out their tangled past, tried to achieve a new relationship in the present, and both times had failed. Yes, perhaps it was time to put it behind him...put her behind him.

For the next two days, he stayed away from the boardwalk, stayed away from her. He worked in the office in his house—a room that had no windows that faced the direction of Land's End. He worked long hours, exhausting hours, hoping that when he finally fell asleep, he would be too tired to dream.

On the third day, he went to the cemetery. He'd arranged to have the area mowed the day before, and decided what he needed was some physical activity to sweat away the memory of Nikki. He'd spend the day weeding and hope the hot sun overhead and the menial labor would exorcise all thoughts, all need for Nikki.

As always, when he approached the tiny grave, a lump jumped in his throat and his eyes burned as if noxious fumes filled the air. He crouched and grabbed a handful of weeds, a sudden oppressive weight filling his chest.

He gasped against the pain, fighting it, not wanting to face it head-on. As he took in deep breaths, battling the grief that threatened to consume him, he found his anger.

Rich and full, it flowed through him, and he embraced it, let it surge through him, fill him up. He stood, wanting to confront Nikki, needing to spill the anger onto her.

He left the cemetery, holding tightly to his anger. This time when he reached her house, his knocks thundered with his rage. "Nikki, it's me.

Nicolette, open the door." He banged against the wood with his fist.

"She isn't there, Grey," Bridget called from the porch next door.

"Where is she?"

Bridget shrugged. "She left yesterday, said she needed some time away from here."

Grey advanced toward Bridget, who was clad in a fuzzy pink bathrobe. "She wouldn't have left without telling you where she was going. Where is she, Bridget?"

"Grey, I promised her I wouldn't tell anyone." Bridget worried the belt of her robe.

"She told me you have a cabin. That's where she went, isn't it?" Grey stepped up on the porch and faced her. "Where's the cabin, Bridget?"

Bridget's forehead crinkled with her frown. "I promised, Grey."

"You can either tell me where your cabin is or I'll spend the next couple of days searching county records to find the location of the cabin you own. But sooner or later, I'll find it and sooner or later I will talk to Nikki. If you tell me now, you'll just be expediting the inevitable." He felt a surge of triumph as Bridget heaved a sigh of resignation.

Within minutes, Grey was driving toward the cabin, his anger still coursing through him. How dare she? How dare she make judgments concerning his emotions. How dare she tell him he didn't care, didn't feel the pain of loss. How self-righteous she had become, wrapping her grief around her like a shroud to keep him from getting too close.

They'd allowed a lack of communication to rip them apart years ago. He wasn't about to let history repeat itself. They were going to talk again, only this time he wouldn't stand and stare at her numbly. This time, she was going to listen to him.

It was nearly dusk when he finally arrived at the cabin. Snuggled amid a canopy of pine trees, the small structure radiated peace and tranquility. Grey felt anything but as he strode purposely to the front door. His knock echoed his heartbeat, resounding in the stillness of the golden-shadowed twilight.

She opened the door, her eyes flaring in surprise, her body tensing at the sight of him. "What are you doing here?" she asked, maintaining a firm grasp on the doorknob.

"You said everything you needed to say the other day. Now it's my turn to say what I need to."

"There's nothing left to say," she protested.

He shoved past her, into the interior of the tiny cabin. "You may have nothing more to say, but I have plenty. Sit down."

She hesitated, gazing out the door as if contemplating running out, away from him. "Please, Nikki," he said softly.

She paused another long moment, then closed the door and sat down on the sofa, her eyes guarded as she looked at him.

Grey stared at her, his anger seeping away as other emotions battled inside. He'd known all that he wanted to say to her before he'd arrived here. But now, the emotion-thick words clogged his throat, expanded in his chest and pressed with a familiar, oppressive weight.

He turned away from her and ran a hand through his hair, trying to find the courage, the heart to face his inner turmoil. "You've had seven years," he finally began, his voice trembling despite his struggle for control. "Seven years to deal with Lolly's... birth and death. And how self-righteous you've become, hugging your grief to yourself, sure that nobody else feels it." To his horror, he felt his eyes burning with the sting of unshed tears. He grabbed inwardly for control, realized in terror that it was gone.

He looked at her once again, his vision blurry as the ball of emotions in his chest shattered, sending grief and torment sweeping through him. "I've had a matter of weeks to face the birth and death of my daughter... to face the fact that had I been there, had I known, things might have been different. Lolly might have lived." The last words were choked out and he covered his face, deep sobs racking his body with frightening intensity.

Nikki felt the shield around her heart shatter and fall away. His sobs were a terrifying, horrible thing to hear, his grief reached inside and tore at her as she felt her own rising to meet his.

"Grey... oh, Grey." She stood and wrapped her arms around him, then led him back to the sofa where they sat down and she cradled him against her.

His scent, so familiar, so beloved, surrounded her, engulfed her. His sobs held a torment too strong to bear.

As she held him, she realized she'd been unfair to him. She had been self-righteous, pompous with her mourning. She'd never considered the fact that the grieving process was different for both of them, different in time, different in response.

He was right, she'd had seven years to mourn and he'd had only a matter of weeks. She'd expected him to be where she was emotionally, had been angry because he wasn't filling her need to talk about Lolly. She simply hadn't considered that he wasn't at that place yet. She'd been consumed with her needs, her emotions, her grief... and she'd never even thought of his.

Twilight deepened to night as she held him. She held him while he cried. She held him while she cried. Together they mourned their loss until there were no more tears left to spend.

"God, I feel so silly, so weak," he said as he moved out of her arms a long while later.

"And to me you've never seemed so strong," Nikki said, tracing the lines on his face with the tip of her finger. It was true, never had he seemed stronger than at this moment, with the tears for his daughter still damp on his face.

"I just wish . . . I just wish . . . ."

"I know," Nikki said softly. "But Grey, even if you had been here, nothing would have been different." She looked into his eyes, saw the guilt that changed them from their charcoal gray to a deeper, sadder shade.

"Dr. Vendricks is a good doctor and he did everything possible to try to save her. There was nothing anyone could do. Lolly's soul wasn't ours to keep and nothing you could have done would have changed that." She saw his guilt abate somewhat and again she traced the lines around his sensual mouth. "Let it all go, Grey. Lolly wouldn't want you to feel guilty and neither do I."

He squeezed his eyes tightly closed, released a tremulous sigh of emotion. "From the moment you told me about her, I've shoved all thoughts of her aside, afraid that facing the loss would make me crazy." He opened his eyes and gazed at her, a fire flickering there. "I need to hold you, Nikki. I need to make love to you now."

Nikki nodded. She understood his need, the desire to share their love as they had finally shared their grief, the need to leave their mourning behind and find a new kind of peace in the shelter of each other's arms.

She stood and held out her hand to him, then led him into the small bedroom. The moonlight shone in through the window and created dancing patterns on the walls. It radiated enough light so she could see the want reflected in his eyes, saw the trembling of his hands as he reached for her.

She went willingly into his arms, needing him as much as he did her. When he kissed her, his lips held the salty remnants of his recent tears and it only made her want him more. They'd mourned their loss together, cried together...now it was time to celebrate love and life together.

She broke their kiss only long enough to step away from him and discard her clothing. He did the same, then swept her up in his arms and carried her to the bed.

He deposited her gently, tenderly, his gaze smoke and flame as it lingered on her. Then he was next to her, his body heat surrounding her as his mouth hungrily consumed hers.

For the first time since his return to the boardwalk, Nikki came to him with her heart healed, her soul completely open to him.

As his mouth claimed hers, her hands moved down his back, as if memorizing the strength of the muscles, the smooth skin that was warm beneath her fingertips. She loved him. She loved him with every fiber of her being, with every aspect of her soul.

He caressed her slowly, languidly, then moved to possess her entirely. As he entered her, filling her body, stroking her very soul, she realized the magic was back. She loved him with a depth and breadth that overwhelmed her and brought tears of joy to her eyes. As he began to move within her, she gazed up at him, her heart surging as she saw the tears of love that glistened in his eyes.

They loved each other as they never had before, with the innocence and wonder of their youth, yet with the wisdom and experience of their maturity.

The magic of rightness, of belonging surged through Nikki and she knew she would never be entirely whole without this man in her life. He'd been right when he'd told her that the magic had never been the boardwalk...it had always been them together.

Afterward, they remained in each other's arms, reluctant to break the embrace. Their bodies had been sated, but it was as if their hearts were still hungry, still needed the closeness of body and spirit.

Nikki lay with her head on his chest, contented with the sound of his heart beating sure and strong against her ear.

"Nikki?"

She smiled at the way his chest vibrated as he softly spoke her name. "Hmm?" She didn't move except to sweep her hand back and forth in the springy hair on his chest.

"What did she look like?"

The soft words stopped the movement of her hand, seemed for a moment to stop the beating of her heart. She raised her head and looked at him, saw the sad regret that darkened his eyes. It was a sadness they would both carry for a very long time, but it was one they would both survive.

"She was beautiful, Grey. Absolutely perfect." She reached up and touched a strand of his midnight-dark hair. "She had a headful of black curls and a mouth wide and full like mine." Nikki smiled softly, surprised to realize that somehow in crying with Grey, some of the deep, painful grief was gone. And with the waning of grief came complete forgiveness and a peace she hadn't known before. "She was the best of us, Grey... the best of us both."

"Oh, Nikki, I love you," he murmured, his mouth moving to kiss her, communicating the words he'd just spoken. "I wish I would have been here with you, for you. I wish I would have been beside you to share the sadness, hold you tight, shoulder at least part of your grief.''

She smiled again, moving her fingers from his hair to his mouth, tracing the sensual lips she loved. ''Better seven years late than never.''

He tightened his arms around her. ''I don't ever want you to go through another bad experience in your life without me. I don't want you to spend another minute of your life without me.'' His voice was fervent, his gaze intense. ''Marry me, Nikki. I only half exist when I'm away from you. Marry me and make me whole.''

Nikki closed her eyes, tears once again burning hotly. Only this time the tears were happy ones. She knew she was only a half without him, and the fact that he felt that way too filled her with an intense happiness.

''Oh, yes, I'll marry you.'' There was no hesitation, no uncertainty. Suddenly, she knew destiny had planned for them to be together long ago, when they'd first pledged their love to each other in the shadows under the boardwalk.

He kissed her. This time, his kiss was not hungry and demanding, but soft, tender, his lips communicating a love to last a lifetime.

Again he snuggled her close to his side, his hand stroking her hair as his heart matched the rhythm of her own. ''We'll plan a ceremony on the carousel,'' he said. ''And that big silver steed with the blue ribbons will be my best man.''

Nikki smiled, imagining in her mind the wedding to come, the ceremony that would bind them legally as their hearts were already bound. ''We're going to have a wonderful life together,'' she said.

''We'll build a house on the beach, here at Land's End. A big house that will be filled with magic and love.''

Nikki laughed at his exuberance, his sheer euphoria. He hugged her once again and laughed out loud. ''Oh God, I feel good. I feel like my life is just beginning.''

''I feel the same way,'' Nikki replied. She felt as if she were seventeen again and were being given a second chance to get it all right.

''And later, if we decide we want children, we can always adopt,'' he continued. ''If you want to we'll adopt a half a dozen kids who will grow up to believe in the magic of love and Land's End.''

''We don't have to adopt,'' Nikki said. For the first time since learning of her pregnancy, her heart swelled with the miracle of it. She blossomed with a joy untainted by fear and anger, unspoiled by bitterness and grief.

She was pregnant with Grey's child. And this would be a child they would share from the very beginning, a child they would raise together, love together. For a moment her emotions clogged her throat, making it impossible for her to speak.

"I know no child could ever replace our Lolly, but you want children, don't you?" He shifted positions so that he had a full view of her face. "Nikki?"

"Oh, yes, I want children, lots of children," she said breathlessly, "but Grey, we don't have to adopt."

"What do you mean?" His brow wrinkled in curiosity.

"I'm pregnant." The words exploded out of her and she watched the play of emotions on his face. His eyes widened in disbelief, the disbelief mingling with a tentative joy.

He sat up, staring down at her. "Are you sure? I thought you couldn't... I thought... the doctor said...." he sputtered in confusion.

"So did I." She laughed. "Dr. Vendricks was as shocked as I was. He said it was nothing short of a miracle."

"A miracle," he echoed, his charcoal eyes caressing her features. The disbelief fell away, replaced by awe. "Our miracle. A baby. We're going to have a baby." He reached out and his hand reverently rubbed the flatness of her abdomen.

He moved his hand from her stomach to her cheek, his touch loving and whisper soft. "A baby," he repeated slowly. Again tears filled his eyes, only this time his smile told her they were happy tears. "The real miracle, Nikki, is us. We're the miracle, the magic, the love. And this time I intend to follow up on a promise I made to you long ago."

"And what was that?" she asked breathless as she felt herself falling into the passion, the glory, the love in his eyes.

He gathered her against him, his arms enfolding her as he kissed her. The hunger was back, a hunger she knew would always exist between them. "Forever," he whispered.

"Forever," she echoed, knowing this time it was a promise that would be fulfilled forever.

* * * * *

Cruel Legacy

One man's untimely *death deprives a wife of her husband, robs a man of his job and offers someone else the chance of a lifetime...*

Suicide — the only way out for Andrew Ryecart, facing crippling debt. An end to his troubles, but for those he leaves behind the problems are just beginning, as the repercussions of this most desperate of acts reach out and touch the lives of six different people — changing them forever.

Special large-format paperback edition

**OCTOBER
£8.99**

W❂RLDWIDE

COMING NEXT MONTH

TEMPTATION TEXAS STYLE!
Annette Broadrick

Man of the Month and *Sons of Texas*

Tony Callaway wasn't pleased when Christina O'Reilly turned up on his ranch. He had no time for *very* distant relatives—or for finding *this* kissing cousin so very kissable!

WOLFE WANTING
Joan Hohl

Big Bad Wolfe

Royce Wolfe was just doing his job—sleeping in Megan's house and making sure she was safe. The problem was that he wanted her badly—and that was the last thing she needed…

THE DADDY FACTOR
Kelly Jamison

When Neal Corrigan turned up at the camp for handicapped children, Charlotte realised that there were pleasures beyond motherhood and career—forbidden pleasures. But she didn't know about Neal's secret mission…

COMING NEXT MONTH

BABIES ON THE DOORSTEP
Raye Morgan

Brittanny never expected to find a basketful of babies on her doorstep—any more than she expected her neighbour, confirmed bachelor Mitchell Caine, to help her look after them…

FIND HER, KEEP HER
Anne Marie Winston

Dane Hamilton needed a wife—quickly! And lonely widow Annie Evans didn't think twice about accepting his proposal. All she was missing now was a baby…and, of course, love…

THE MATING GAME
Susan Crosby

Hot sand and the advances of sexy Iain MacKenzie were just what Kani needed. She didn't know that they hadn't met by chance—or that she'd been designated his future wife…

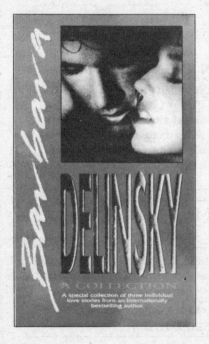

GET 4 BOOKS
AND A MYSTERY GIFT

Return the coupon below and we'll send you 4 Silhouette Desires and mystery gift absolutely FREE! We'll even pay the postage and packing for you.

We're making you this offer to introduce you to the benefits of Reader Service: FREE home delivery of brand-new Silhouette romances, at least a month before they are available in the shops, FREE gifts and a monthly Newsletter packed with information.

Accepting these FREE books and gift places you under no obligation to buy, you may cancel at any time, even after receiving just your free shipment. Simply complete the coupon below and send it to:

HARLEQUIN MILLS & BOON, FREEPOST, PO BOX 70, CROYDON, CR9 9EL.

COMING NEXT MONTH FROM

 **SILHOUETTE**

Sensation

A thrilling mix of passion, adventure and drama

BETWEEN ROC AND A HARD PLACE
Heather Graham Pozzessere
McLAIN'S LAW Kylie Brant
HIS OTHER MOTHER Suzette Vann
SECRETS Jennifer Greene

Intrigue

*Danger, deception and desire—
new from Silhouette...*

NO HOLDS BARRED Patricia Rosemoor
WHISPERS IN THE NIGHT Rebecca York
STOLEN MEMORIES Kelsey Roberts
LOOKS ARE DECEIVING Maggie Ferguson

Special Edition

Satisfying romances packed with emotion

BABIES ON BOARD Gina Ferris
A IS FOR ALWAYS Lisa Jackson
BACHELOR DAD Carole Halston
AN INTERRUPTED MARRIAGE Laurey Bright
HESITANT HERO Christina Dair
HIGH COUNTRY COWBOY Sandra Moore